STAR WARS
THE
MANDALORIAN

JUNIOR NOVEL

Adapted by Joe Schreiber

Based on the series created by Jon Favreau and written by
Jon Favreau, Dave Filoni, Christopher Yost, and Rick Famuyiwa

DISNEY
LUCASFILM
PRESS

Los Angeles • New York

© & TM 2021 Lucasfilm Ltd.

All rights reserved. Published by Disney • Lucasfilm Press, an imprint of
Buena Vista Books, Inc. No part of this book may be reproduced or transmitted
in any form or by any means, electronic or mechanical, including photocopying,
recording, or by any information storage and retrieval system, without written
permission from the publisher.

For information address Disney • Lucasfilm Press,
1200 Grand Central Avenue, Glendale, California 91201.

Printed in the United States of America

First Edition, January 2021

1 3 5 7 9 10 8 6 4 2

FAC-029261-20332

ISBN 978-1-368-05713-4

Library of Congress Control Number on file

Reinforced binding

Visit the official *Star Wars* website at: www.starwars.com.

A long time ago in a galaxy far,
far away. . . .

CHAPTER

"IT'S MY HIGHEST bounty," Greef Karga said.

From his side of the table, the Mandalorian looked back at him. It was never clear whether Karga was telling the whole truth. In the man's role as a local agent for the Bounty Hunters Guild, he scattered half-truths, rumors, and outright lies the same way he used Imperial credits and bounty pucks—as tools of maintaining some uneasy, ever-shifting balance among the hunters he worked with and the shadowy figures he served. It was nothing personal, just business.

"Let's see the puck," Mando said, referring to the small holographic device that contained information about the bounty.

"No puck. Face to face." Karga paused. "Direct commission. Deep pocket."

The Mandalorian wasn't surprised. Often the most profitable work came with the least amount of information, usually for the protection of the client, who didn't want their business known to the public. "Underworld?"

"All I know is there's no chain code," Karga said, not bothering to hide his impatience. "Do you want the chit or not?"

The Mandalorian took it. It was never really a question. Even for an experienced hunter like himself, whose reputation preceded him, pickings were slim, from the Core Worlds to the Outer Rim. After the fall of the Empire, the galaxy seemed to have lost its way. There was little economic stability or rule of law, and if the New Republic's promise of peace and prosperity had yet come to pass, it hadn't trickled its way down to a backwater planet like Nevarro. On those streets and a thousand others like them, smugglers and thieves, local warlords and thugs all conducted their business in the shadows, and sometimes even in broad daylight. More and more of the time, crime flourished, but for bounty hunters, the criminals themselves were worth less and less.

As he walked along the back streets, on his way to meet his new client, Mando thought about the immediate future—his next assignment, and the next, and the one after that. Countless faces, forgotten planets, their names reduced to credits paid and owed. These targets formed a chain of their own, an endless stream of bounties extending off into some uncertain future. The Guild expected hunters to bring their bounty in with no questions asked, and forgetting about it just as quickly afterward was part of the trade, which suited the Mandalorian just fine.

He already had too much he couldn't forget.

The roar of explosions, the terrified faces of his parents, gleaming with sweat—all of it still vivid and jarring—as they rushed with him through the street, their entire world falling to pieces behind them in the Great Purge—

Beyond it all was the Creed.

Somewhere between the darkness of the past and the vague blur of the future, the road itself remained clear. Wherever he went, the skills and strength of the Mandalorians provided the path beneath his feet, a destiny that would always be waiting for him.

It was the Way.

CHAPTER

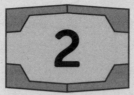

"GREEF KARGA SAID you were coming."

Mando stood in front of the Client, letting the silence play out around him. For a supposed safe house, the room didn't feel particularly safe. Walking in, he'd found four stormtroopers in dusty, battle-scarred armor surrounding him, blasters at the ready. Like the Empire they once served, the troopers had been stripped of their official authority but not of their menace. These days, they worked, fought, and killed for whoever offered the highest pay.

"What else did Karga say?" Mando asked.

"He said you were the best in the parsec." The Client's expression didn't change. He was a man in his seventies with white hair and an accent Mando couldn't place, but his distinguished mannerisms hinted at a former life as a highly ranked Imperial officer. "He also said you were expensive."

It wasn't a question, and Mando didn't bother to answer it. There was a muffled clink as he watched the old man unfold a piece of soft black fabric across the table in front of him to reveal a flat rectangular plate of metal lying at the center of the red lining. He was aware of the troopers behind him leaning in for a closer look. Even they couldn't disguise their interest in such a treasure. The Mandalorian knew its name at once.

"Beskar?"

"This is only a down payment," the Client said. "The rest will be waiting for you on delivery of the asset."

"Alive," added the anxious, bespectacled man standing next to him. The Client had introduced him as Dr. Pershing, and the doctor's excited entrance into the room a moment earlier had nearly gotten him shot before the Client had asked Mando to put away his blaster.

"Proof of termination is also acceptable, for a lower fee," the Client said, not bothering to acknowledge Pershing's sputtering objections. "I'm simply being practical. Bounty hunting is an uncertain business." The old man waited, allowing the meaning of the words to sink in. "The beskar belongs back with a Mandalorian. It is good to restore the natural order of things after a period of such disarray." He raised his eyes upward. "Don't you agree?"

Agree or not, the job was his, and the beskar with it. The Client had provided him with a tracking fob and the quarry's last known location. The hunt awaited.

But first he needed to make one more stop.

He stepped through the hidden doorway and followed the steps down into the coolness and familiarity of the shadows that awaited him. The Armorer's foundry was down a long flight of stairs, located deep beneath the surface, hidden away from the eyes of the enemies that had driven their sect underground. This was a secret place, its location carefully guarded. There in the gloom, the steady circle of blue flames burned brightly, and the clink of the Armorer's hammer gave the darkness a kind of heartbeat all its own.

He and the Armorer exchanged nods, and when he gave the bar of beskar to her, she didn't speak immediately.

"This was gathered in the Great Purge," she eventually said. "It is good that it is back with the tribe." She looked at him. "A pauldron would be in order. Has your signet been revealed?"

"No."

"Soon." As she melted the beskar down in the forge, the molten metal streaming through a series of heated troughs to fill the waiting mold, her voice softened somewhat. "This is extremely generous. The excess will sponsor many foundlings."

"That's good," Mando said. "I was once a foundling."

"I know," she said, and there was little more to add to the conversation.

Soon enough, he was on his way.

CHAPTER

THE *RAZOR CREST* WAS HOME.

Where others might look at the gunship and see a simple means of transportation or escape, the Mandalorian knew the *Crest* as his haven, almost an extension of the armor and helmet that protected him. Programming the navicomputer with the coordinates provided by the Client, he felt the familiar rumble of thrusters taking hold, deepening through the gunship's frame as it broke away from the spaceport, tilted slightly on its axis, and flung itself into space.

In many ways, the pursuit of his quarry was always the same. It was only a matter of time before he returned to Nevarro with his bounty in tow, he collected what was owed, and then the whole process began again.

And yet this time felt different.

Perhaps it was seeing the beskar, feeling its weight in his hands, and hearing the Armorer's prediction that his signet would soon be revealed.

The ship flew on for some time, arcing across space, until a proximity beacon began to pulse on the console in front of him. His senses sharpened as he leaned in to switch the navigation back over to manual. Arvala-7 was the name of the planet—its rocky landscape spreading out before him in barren, jagged peaks as he dropped his altitude and began his initial descent.

The desert rose up to meet him, gradually then all at once. Extending the landing gear, he brought the ship down in a flat canyon surrounded by reddish-brown foothills, then stepped out and walked down the boarding ramp to survey the land, the tracking fob blinking in his hand. After hours spent inside the ship, it felt good to stand on solid ground, even if the soil itself felt muddy and soft beneath his boots.

He raised his rifle, activated the scope, and took his time scanning the wide-open landscape, tracking the line of the horizon until he settled on a pair of squat, two-legged creatures wandering across the plain. The things were almost absurdly ugly, round-backed with blunt heads like primitive fish and mouths full of teeth that looked like they could easily crush whatever they could catch. No doubt they were dangerous up close—although the Mandalorian was determined to keep his distance. For the time being, he only saw two of them.

The third was standing right in front of him.

———

The creature attacked him with a snarling bellow. Mando screamed as it clamped its jaws around his arm, jerked him off his feet, and threw him to the ground. When he managed to break free and blast it with his flamethrower, the beast squawked and released him just long enough for him to realize that he'd only made it angry. Within moments, another of its kind had arrived and would almost certainly have finished him off if not for the tranquilizer darts that suddenly dropped both creatures to the ground.

Mando looked up and saw another one of the creatures lumbering forward. Unlike the others, this one carried a rider—an Ugnaught in flier's goggles and helmet who seemed unsurprised to find a Mandalorian sprawled on the ground with his leg trapped underneath one of the beasts.

Mando nodded at the tranquilizer darts embedded in the creatures' skin. "Thank you."

The Ugnaught observed him for a moment with the gaze of one who was used to spending his days alone. "You are a bounty hunter."

"Yes."

"I am Kuiil," he said. "I will help you."

I didn't ask for your help, Mando thought, but the Ugnaught had already nodded.

"I have spoken."

CHAPTER

4

KUIL INFORMED the Mandalorian that the creatures that had attacked him were called blurrgs. They were ugly and smelled horrible, but if the Mandalorian was going to travel on Arvala-7, he would not only need to ride one but also must learn to do so with some degree of mastery.

"Many have passed through here," Kuiil told him as they sat in his encampment, discussing the trip. "They seek the same one as you."

"Did you help them?"

"Yes." The Ugnaught poured water into a cup and held it out, offering it to him. "They died."

"Then I don't know if I want your help."

Kuiil didn't bother to argue.

Later that afternoon, Kuiil took the bounty hunter out to the paddock behind his compound and watched patiently as his new guest mounted a blurrg and was thrown off, over and over again. Kuiil wondered how much the Mandalorian's armor cushioned the blows. From where he was standing, Mando's struggles looked brutal and didn't seem to be getting any better. The blurrg was the first one Kuiil had shot earlier with a tranquilizer dart, and he had to admit the beast seemed to be in an even worse mood than before, determined to exact revenge for the Mandalorian's attempt to roast it with his flamethrower.

Perhaps you shouldn't have been so quick with that weapon, Kuiil thought, but he decided to keep his opinion to himself. Standing on the other side of the fence, he didn't need to see the Mandalorian's face behind the visor to know that the hunter was growing more exasperated every time the blurrg threw him off. His patience had clearly worn thin.

"I don't have time for this," Mando said. "Do you have a landspeeder or a speeder bike that I could hire?"

Kuiil shook his head. "You are a Mandalorian!" he said. "Your ancestors rode the great mythosaurs! Surely you can ride this young foal."

The Mandalorian staggered to his feet and looked across the paddock, where the blurrg was glaring back at him with baleful yellow eyes, already preparing for their next match. Kuiil, who knew the creature's expression well, felt as though he could almost read the blurrg's thoughts. *I will defeat you,* her eyes said. *I have thrown far better men than you to the ground, bounty hunter, and I will do so again, long after you are gone from this place. Unless of course you choose to die here.*

Kuiil waited to see what the bounty hunter would do—give up and walk away, or make another attempt to subdue the blurrg by force?

But the Mandalorian did neither. At first, he seemed to do nothing at all. Kuiil watched as he took one tentative step toward the blurrg, arms at his sides, hands slightly outstretched in a gesture of peace, and then another step. "Easy," he said, and this time, instead of throwing himself at the creature, he moved toward her slowly, allowing her time to adjust to his presence. "Okay."

The creature snuffed and grunted at him, but didn't charge. By the time he reached her, she had allowed him to place his hand on the top of her head. "All right," Mando said, and pulled himself up onto her back. She growled but didn't try to throw him, and by the time they'd left the paddock, heading into the open desert, he'd begun to find his balance.

Leaving the camp, Mando and Kuiil rode single file upward into higher country, along a series of peaks and narrow ridges interspersed with crevasses so deep they couldn't see the bottom. The blurrgs leapt over these gaps in the earth with surprising agility, never losing their footing. Moving down into flatter terrain, the two riders advanced across vast baked plates of dirt that seemed to have fractured, broken in a way that would never heal, as they dried under the remorseless eye of the sun.

Finally, reaching a high plateau, Kuiil brought his mount to heel and pointed down. "That is where you'll find your quarry."

Gazing at the compound below, Mando reached into the side pouch of his harness and pulled out a small bag of credits. "Please," he told Kuiil. "You deserve this."

The Ugnaught shook his head. "Since these ones arrived, this territory has been an endless stream of mercenaries seeking reward and bringing destruction," he said. "I grow weary of it."

Mando looked at him, not understanding. "Then why did you guide me?"

"They do not belong here," Kuiil said. "Those that live here come to seek peace. There'll be no peace until they're gone."

"Then why did you help me?"

Kuiil didn't respond right away. Years of having no one to talk to had made him mindful of his words, and he chose them with care. "I have never met a Mandalorian," he said. "I've only read the stories. If they are true, then you will make quick work of it. Then there will again be peace." Tugging at the reins of his mount, he raised one hand in a gesture of finality. "I have spoken."

CHAPTER

5

THE CAMP WAS a U-shaped arrangement of flat-roofed buildings around a dusty open plaza. Looking down through his viewing scope, Mando observed the Nikto mercenaries and guards passing time in the late afternoon sun. Accustomed to the desert environment, the Nikto were scaly-skinned and imposing, their faces and heads studded with horns and spikes. To him, they looked dangerous in the way the renegade stormtroopers at the safe house had been dangerous—like bored soldiers, heavily armed and looking for trouble.

He was still watching them, planning his approach, when an immediately recognizable mechanized figure walked into the compound and made the situation worse.

"Attention," the bounty droid said to the mercenaries. It was an IG unit, designed for combat. "Subparagraph sixteen of the Bondsman Guild protocol waiver compels you to immediately produce said asset."

"Oh, no," Mando muttered. Down below, the IG was still moving forward when the guards around the plaza reached for their blasters—and simultaneously signed their death warrants. Without hesitating, the droid snapped into action, spinning around and opening fire on the gunman directly in front of it, its body turning effortlessly with blasters in either hand, firing nonstop with precision-tooled accuracy. Not once did it falter, even when a blaster bolt ricocheted off its processor plate.

As Mando made his way down the escarpment and into the compound, he was aware that the blasting had ceased. Silence filled the open space. By the time the last echoes had faded and the smoke and dust had settled, he saw that the ground was covered with the bodies of the hired Nikto. In the quiet, the droid's voice sounded exactly the same as it had before, completely unflappable, as it repeated its mission.

"Subparagraph sixteen of the Bondsman Guild protocol waiver compels you to immediately produce said asset," it said, and advanced forward with the unswerving confidence that was a unique quality of bounty droids.

Mando moved around the corner. "IG unit, stand down!"

The droid shot him. The Mandalorian felt the blaster bolt smash into his breastplate, the force of the impact powerful enough to throw him backward into a row of barrels lined up along the wall behind him. At the same moment, pain slashed through his shoulder and down his rib cage, and he fought to catch his breath. The beskar had deflected the worst of the shot, but there would be plenty of pain in his immediate future.

In front of him, the droid was watching, perhaps still processing why its blaster hadn't done more damage. Mando sat up, realizing he might have less than a second to convince the IG to hold off on finishing him with a head shot.

"I'm in the Guild!" he shouted, holding up the tracking fob.

"You are a Guild member?" For the first time, the droid's voice revealed a note of uncertainty. "I am IG-11," it added with professional courtesy. "I thought I was the only one on assignment."

"That makes two of us." Mando turned to survey the fortified entrance in front of them. No doubt there were more of the Nikto inside, all of them fully aware that something outside had gone very wrong. "So much for the element of surprise."

But the IG had more pressing matters to discuss. "Sadly, I must ask for your fob. The bounty is mine."

The Mandalorian looked at the droid, weighing his options. "Unless I am mistaken," he said, "you are as yet empty-handed."

"This is true."

"I have a suggestion," Mando said.

"Proceed."

"We split the reward."

Without hesitation, the IG replied: "This is acceptable."

"Great," Mando said. "Now let's regroup, out of harm's way, and form a plan."

If the droid had an answer, he didn't hear it.

That was when the second wave hit.

There were more of the Nikto this time, spilling out of the shadows and onto the rooftops, raining down blaster fire from all directions. Ducking for cover, the Mandalorian shot back and watched as the IG pivoted and fired bolt after bolt. Every shot was a direct hit, thanks to its programming—but even so, the situation was rapidly slipping out of control. More and more Nikto kept appearing. After a certain point, Mando and IG-11 would be too outnumbered.

Mando checked the tracking fob. Its signal was intensifying. He glanced across the plaza at the closed gate. No mistake: the asset was in there. They were so close. But twenty meters away, under a steady hail of blaster fire, they might as well have been on the other side of Wild Space.

"It appears we are trapped," the droid said, seemingly programmed to state the obvious. "I will initiate self-destruct sequencing."

"Whoa!" The Mandalorian whirled around, wondering if he'd heard properly. "You're what?"

"Manufacturer's protocol dictates I cannot be captured. I must self-destruct."

"Do not self-destruct!" Mando ordered. "Cover me!"

Apparently willing to entertain this alternative, at least temporarily, the IG whirled around and continued firing while the bounty hunter ducked and ran across the plaza to the entry point. There was an outdated security panel with an access pad, and given time and the absence of blaster fire, he might've been able to run a bypass, but right then there wasn't enough of either. A second later, a blaster bolt struck the panel and reduced it to a sizzling pan of wires and circuitry.

"They've got us pinned!" he shouted.

"I will initiate self-destruct sequence," the droid announced cheerfully.

"Do not self-destruct! We're shooting our way out!"

But something had changed in the attitude of the Nikto surrounding them. They had paused and were looking back over their shoulders. When the Mandalorian followed their line of sight, he saw what had caught their attention—a heavy-artillery laser cannon mounted on a hover pad was being pushed into position across the plaza, its massive barrel aimed directly at him and the droid.

"Okay," Mando said. "New plan. We—"

The cannon roared, spitting a massive hail of fire. Thanks

to the cannon's hover mount, its operator had an unlimited range, and the Mandalorian knew that the weapon packed enough firepower that one direct hit would be more than any amount of armor could handle. Somewhere in the background, he heard the IG announcing that it was, once again, initiating its self-destruct protocols.

"Draw their fire!" Mando shouted. "I'll take it out!"

"Acceptable," the droid replied, and stepped out into the open. Immediately, the laser cannon's operator focused the attack on IG-11, hammering its reinforced body with a nonstop volley of blaster fire. Mando couldn't help admiring it. Droid or not, it didn't hesitate to put itself directly in harm's way when the situation called for it.

He slipped forward, taking advantage of the diversion to move low and quickly through the shadows around the back of the cannon's operator while the IG continued to take heavy fire and eventually dropped to the ground. From his current position, Mando saw the opportunity he'd created and took advantage of it. Raising his wrist gauntlet, he fired a grappling wire into the side of the cannon, pulled the wire taut, and yanked it hard enough to spin the entire hover platform around, hurling the surprised gunman from his perch.

Now! Go!

The bounty hunter jumped onto the platform, grabbed the cannon, took hold of the triggers, and squeezed. Spinning, he opened fire on the remaining Nikto, the weapon pulsing in his grasp as they fell in waves. Within seconds, it was over, the last of them defeated.

"Well done," the IG said. "I will disengage self-destruct initiative."

Mando walked over and extended his hand, helping the IG to its feet. "You know, you're not so bad," he said. "For a droid."

"Agreed."

"That blaster hit looks nasty." He glanced at the droid's carbon-scored metallic chest plates. "You okay?"

The IG ran a quick diagnostic and confirmed that the shot had missed its central neural harness. The Mandalorian nodded, took a breath, and glanced down at the tracker.

"Well," he said, "now all we have to do is get that door open."

He and the IG stood for a moment, and then they both looked back at the cannon.

CHAPTER

6

AS EXPECTED, the cannon made short work of the security gate. After a series of direct hits, the whole thing gave way with a thundering crash.

Mando stood for a moment in the doorway, looking inside. The air smelled old and stale. Dust swirled in the shafts of light streaming from above and falling on the storage crates and packaging scattered randomly against the walls. Aside from the Nikto, there was no sense of who else had been living there, what exactly they'd used the place for, or if there were any stragglers remaining.

As if summoned by the unspoken question, a lone Nikto sprang out from around the corner, blaster in hand. The Mandalorian fired, hardly pausing to aim, and the guard flew backward and hit the floor.

"Anyone else?"

Silence, except for the beep of the tracking fob. The IG

turned to him. "My sensors indicate that there is a life-form present."

Mando held the tracker in front of him, walking forward as the beeping intensified, following the signal until he found himself looking at a silver egg-shaped container hovering just above the floor. Leaning down, he tapped a release button, and the cover sprang open to reveal a small shape partially covered by a blanket.

For a moment he just looked at it. The creature raised a small, three-fingered hand and pulled down the blanket to reveal its green face, the tiny mouth and nose set beneath large, watchful eyes and ears so long they almost touched the inside edges of the vessel where it lay cradled. The mouth opened, and Mando heard something like a soft cooing noise, the sound of a very small child who hadn't yet learned how to use language.

"Wait," the Mandalorian said. "They said it was fifty years old."

"Species age differently," the IG remarked. "Perhaps it could live many centuries." It raised its blaster. "Sadly, we'll never know."

"No," Mando said, stopping the droid. "We'll bring it in alive."

"The commission was quite specific. The asset was to be terminated."

Mando looked at the droid, sensing its resolve—a simple

matter of programming, nothing to be bargained with—and considered his options. The decision didn't take long. He raised his blaster and fired a single point-blank shot through the IG's cranial vault, dropping the droid to the floor. A thin ribbon of smoke rose from the hole in its steel plating. Lowering the blaster, Mando turned back to the hover pram, then held out one hand to the creature gazing up at him.

It raised its finger to his and touched it.

A moment later, they walked out of the safe house and stepped into the light.

CHAPTER

7

IN HIS YEARS as a bounty hunter, the Mandalorian had gone after all manner of quarry—some violent, others timid, some charismatic and seemingly friendly—but never had he encountered anything quite like this . . . child.

If it even is a child, he thought. Fifty years old, yes, but still, the IG's words echoed through his mind: *Species age differently.* Mando found himself looking back at the thing, trying to figure it out. Everything about the way it gazed up at him with a mixture of curiosity, wonder, and trust indicated that it was still very young, perhaps even an infant. But there was cleverness behind those eyes.

As he walked, the hover pram floated along not far behind him. They made their way across the plaza toward the escarpment, to the place where the mountains bulked jaggedly against the reddening horizon. Looking ahead, the Mandalorian already found himself thinking about the Client, back on Nevarro, and what possible use the man might have for this most highly prized asset. Of course the galaxy was crawling with valuable and deadly things that made themselves appear unremarkable and helpless to take advantage of those who misjudged them.

He looked again at the Child in its pram, floating an arm's length behind him. The Child's eyes gleamed back in his direction, attentive, drinking in the details of the landscape. Perhaps the Client's fascination was more that of a collector of exotic species and he'd wanted this one as an addition to some private menagerie.

But why all the protection? Why was the path to the Child so heavily guarded?

The Mandalorian paused to survey the low, rock-enclosed caverns that stood between him and the way back to his ship. Tiny creatures—the quick, lizard-like gorvin snu—scampered across the rocks. The Child peered at them. Soon it would be dark, and Mando had to figure out how to get back. His blurrg was gone—it must have wandered off at some point to seek its own path—so it appeared they would be making the journey to his ship by foot, which meant—

He paused midstep, listening to the silence. A lonely whistle of wind through the open canyon was followed by the faint but unmistakable rustle of fabric. They weren't alone. A shadow flickered across the rock wall to his immediate left.

He reached down and released the catch on his holster, resting his hand on his blaster.

A second later, the Trandoshan leapt down at him with a snarl, brandishing a vibro-axe. The Mandalorian twisted clear of the blade and reached out to shove the Child's pram as hard as he could, out of harm's way, hearing—could it be?—a faint giggle of delight from inside.

A second Trandoshan sprang out to join the first, both of them swinging axes, roaring and snarling, charging him from either side. Mando flung up his rifle to block the first Trandoshan's attack, but the second came in low with his weapon and connected with Mando's chest. The bite of the blade was deadly sharp, cleaving through his armor and slashing into skin, and the bounty hunter felt a bright lance of pain.

Catching the scent of blood, the assailants doubled their efforts. The Mandalorian managed to knock the legs out from beneath one of them, pivoted, and brought the rifle up swiftly from below. He hit the Trandoshan in front of him with a jolt of electricity and clubbed him across the back of the skull. When the other backed away, spun around, and ran, Mando raised the rifle and fired the disruptor, reducing the runaway to a pile of loose clothing that fluttered to the ground.

But not *just* clothing.

Looking down at the fabric, Mando saw the tracking fob that the Trandoshans had brought with them. More bounty hunters had come to claim their prize. How many of their kind had the Client engaged? A dozen? A hundred?

He drew in another breath. At this point, there was no

reason not to expect more hunters. But with the desert wind rising and night on its way, they needed a place to stop and rest, preferably on higher ground, so he could repair his armor and treat his injuries.

They went on.

Darkness fell with a suddenness that was both surprising and inevitable. By then, the Mandalorian had found a suitable place to stop, activated his lantern, and sat down with a low-voltage cauterizing tool to treat the wounds on his chest and arm. The bite of the vibro-axe had been painful but not particularly deep, and the cauterizer sealed the flesh into a puckered, blackened soon-to-be scar—another in a collection of many.

Glancing up, he saw that the Child had climbed out of his vessel and toddled over with one arm extended, as if he sensed what Mando was doing—the pain he was in, the harshness of the healing process—and wanted to help.

The Mandalorian looked at him and shook his head. "Get back in there."

He picked up the Child and settled him back in the pram. It was almost fully dark, and above them, the first few stars had crept into view, more and more materializing in clusters of light. He abruptly felt very tired.

I'll just close my eyes for a minute.

When he opened them again, it was daylight.

CHAPTER

8

BY THE TIME they reached the *Razor Crest*, it was already too late.

Coming up over the hillside with the pram still floating along behind him, the Mandalorian heard the unmistakable cackle of high-pitched voices that somehow sounded both irritated and jubilant. The language wasn't one that he spoke, but the voices were instantly familiar.

Jawas.

Standing atop the bluff, he gazed down at the small army of brown-hooded forms as they scurried busily around the *Crest*, stripping the parts from his ship and carrying them up the loading ramp of their enormous sandcrawler. As long-time dwellers of the desert, the Jawas considered themselves entitled to whatever they found there, in the same way that wind, sand, and sun might claim dominion over the rest of it.

From the look of things, they'd already loaded a good bit of the *Razor Crest* aboard the sandcrawler.

Leveling his disruptor rifle and aiming it down at the Jawas, Mando picked one at random and squeezed the trigger, watching its brown cloak fly up in the air and flutter empty to the ground. The effect on the rest of the scavenging party was instantaneous. At once, the salvage operation erupted into a general panic, work forgotten and voices squealing as all the other Jawas scrambled for cover. After reloading the disruptor, Mando took his time, picking off two of the slower ones as the rest of the group clambered up the ramp into the sandcrawler, the hatchway slamming shut behind them.

Rising to his feet, the bounty hunter took off running down the cliffside, rifle at the ready. Ahead of him the crawler had already jolted into motion. The vehicle was a fortress, sand-pitted and seemingly ancient, and the most surprising thing about it was how quickly it moved. He ran faster to catch up to it, already gauging the distance, knowing that he needed the parts of his ship that the Jawas had taken, and that he'd do whatever it took to get them back.

Even if it meant scaling the side of the crawler itself.

Mando fired a cable and began to pull himself up the side. The vehicle swerved, heading for a rocky outcropping in the distance. Mando saw the rocks coming and yanked himself tight against a recessed area of the crawler, tucking his body in mere seconds before he would've been crushed. The crawler scraped along the cliffside. He clutched the metal edge of the vehicle, waiting as it passed, before swinging free.

Then he had the space to resume his climb up the side of the crawler, his cape blowing out behind him in the rush of wind. The upward climb was like scaling a metal cliff, but it was the only way. If he could get to the top—

Wham! Something hit him in the shoulder, and he looked up. Rusty metal hatchways were swinging open all over the side of the crawler, and Mando saw Jawas popping their heads out, eyes glowing with malicious glee as they pelted him with bits of debris—a rusty wheel, a droid's leg, a jagged metal sprocket. He ducked and slipped, clinging with only one hand, his feet dangling beneath him as another makeshift projectile whistled past his head, missing him by centimeters.

Mando aimed his free arm above his head and fired the grappling cable straight up. The cable found its mark and wrapped around one of the skinny metal arrays that protruded from the top of the crawler. With a grunt of effort, he started pulling himself up, hand over hand.

More debris came flying down, smacking into his visor. The Jawas' mobile junkyard had no shortage of ammunition. Mando could hear them up there laughing, making a game of it, seeing how many times they could nail him as he climbed. But it wouldn't be long; he was almost—

A hatchway popped open immediately in front of him, and a Jawa leaned out with an electrical prod and jabbed him in the chest. Mando felt the current shoot through him and groaned with pain, dangling helplessly from the cable. He grabbed the Jawa and yanked him loose, hearing the high-pitched wail as he fell.

Reaching the top of the crawler, Mando pulled himself up and drew his blaster.

A dozen Jawas were standing there, ion blasters pointed at him. With a unified cry of victory, they all fired at once, and Mando saw everything go black as he fell backward, down a great distance to more darkness below.

"They threw *salvage* at you?" Kuiil asked. He wasn't surprised, merely intrigued by what he'd just heard. "That's interesting. Usually Jawas aren't so quick to let go of what they've found."

"They were trying to kill me," the Mandalorian said. "I was hanging off the side of their crawler."

It was dusk again, and Kuiil had welcomed the bounty hunter back to his homestead, along with the strange creature he'd brought with him. The Mandalorian had repaid Kuiil for his hospitality with a fascinating story about what happened to him and his ship, and a group of Jawas. Apparently there had been a chase, followed by a mighty battle, which the Mandalorian had clearly lost.

Kuiil had listened to every detail. He was particularly fascinated by the bounty hunter's failed effort to climb up the side of the sandcrawler, dodging the scraps of metal and refuse that the Jawas were pelting down at him. When the Mandalorian told him how he'd finally reached the top of the crawler, only to have a dozen Jawas blast him all at once and fling him back over the side, Kuiil shook his head in amazement. It was a testimony to the bounty hunter's great resilience, as well as the strength of his armor, that he had survived such a fall. Kuiil turned his attention to Mando's bounty, who was currently occupied by a passing frog, and pointed at him.

"This is what was causing all the fuss?" Kuiil asked.

"I think he's a child," Mando said.

Kuiil had never seen anything like him. "Better to deliver it alive then."

"My ship has been destroyed." The Mandalorian made an adjustment to one of the gauntlets on his wrist. "I'm trapped here."

"Stripped," Kuiil corrected, "not destroyed. The Jawas steal, they don't destroy."

"Stolen or destroyed," Mando said, "makes no difference to me. They're protected by their crawling fortress. I'll never recover the parts." Behind him, the bounty—the Child—made an excited, babbling coo as he pounced on the frog he'd been following.

Kuiil had an idea. "You can trade."

"With Jawas?" Mando asked. "Are you out of your mind?"

"I will take you to them," the Ugnaught said, and before the bounty hunter could argue, he added, "I have spoken." He glanced back at the Child and saw that the frog he'd caught was just visible as a pair of long, wiggling legs sticking out of the tiny creature's mouth.

"Hey," Mando said, "spit that out."

Instead, the Child gulped and the legs disappeared down his throat. His only response was a loud burp.

"At least you don't have to worry about feeding it," Kuiil observed. "It seems to find its own food."

"I'm not going to have him with me that long," the Mandalorian said.

Kuiil nodded at the horizon. "If we're going to get your ship back," he said, "we ought to get moving."

They rode all night, across whole stretches of unmapped desert and beneath an electrical storm that flung wild streaks of lightning across the sky. Kuiil led the way astride his blurrg while the Mandalorian followed on an empty lev-loader that they'd brought along with them. The odds of getting anything back from the Jawas seemed slim, but there was no other way off the planet.

By the time they observed the sandcrawler and the Jawa encampment ahead of them in the distance, dawn was breaking and the Jawas had already seen them coming. Kuiil could see them picking up weapons and preparing what appeared to be a counterassault.

"They really don't seem to like you for some reason," the Ugnaught observed.

"Well . . ." The Mandalorian watched as more Jawas popped their heads out of hatches in the sides of the crawler. "I did disintegrate a few of them."

"You need to drop your rifle."

"I'm a Mandalorian. Weapons are part of my religion."

"Then you aren't getting your parts back," Kuiil said.

The bounty hunter sighed. With great reluctance, he set aside his rifle while Kuiil stepped forward, approached the Jawas, and spoke patiently to them, then waited and listened while they responded. He'd been right about one thing: they really didn't like the Mandalorian and were still upset about what he'd done to them. But after a moment more, Kuiil came back with an offer.

"They will trade all the parts for the beskar," he said.

"I'm not trading anything!" Mando snapped. "Those are my parts. They stole them from me!" He turned to them, summoning his rudimentary knowledge of their language: "*Dee-jugg . . . dee-jugg . . . je-jo-so—*"

The Jawas erupted with laughter, mocking his attempts to communicate. "*You speak terrible Jawa,*" the one in front of him jeered. "*You sound like a Wookiee!*"

"You understand *this*?" Mando flung his arm out, the wrist-mounted flamethrower spewing an orange jet of fire that evoked a shriek of fright and surprise from the Jawas as they scrambled backward, no doubt cursing him as they did so.

But Kuiil hadn't given up. He began speaking to the Jawas again, in the same calm and respectful tone, and they actually seemed to be listening. "*Please*," he said. "*There must be something else, something you want, something you would take in trade.*"

This time, the answer came back in words that even the Mandalorian could understand.

"*You must bring us the Egg. We require the Egg.*"

"The Egg?" Mando looked back at Kuiil. "What egg?"

The only answer was that same word, chanted over and over.

"*Egg. Egg. Egg.*"

Kuiil looked at Mando, who was looking back at him, possibly with the same thought.

It was just an egg. How hard could it be?

CHAPTER

9

WHAM!

The Mandalorian went flying backward out of the cave, unsure what had hit him. The thing inside had thrown him straight into the air, and he'd hit the ground with a spine-jarring crash that flattened his lungs and left him momentarily unable to breathe. It had all happened very quickly. The creature whose egg he'd been sent in to retrieve, to trade for the parts to his ship—the Jawa called it a mudhorn—had slammed into him headfirst. It was like colliding with a living wall of muscle and bone.

From the sound of it, the thing was coming out to finish the job.

Mando managed to lift his head, eyes starting to focus, and watched as the beast lumbered out from the stinking darkness of its lair. For a moment he could only stare. The mudhorn was even bigger and deadlier than it had appeared inside the cave. In broad daylight, the massive bone-colored horn sprouting from its shaggy head looked sharp enough to impale whatever it caught. Its matted brown pelt was caked with muck and filth.

It stank of death.

And it was furious.

Mando reached for his rifle. As the thing thundered toward him, he could actually feel the ground shaking under its weight, and he raised the rifle, aimed, pulled the trigger—

But nothing happened. Something had gone wrong. The rifle wouldn't fire. The beast was charging faster, galloping, closing the distance between them—

WHAM!

Again he was airborne, and this time when he hit the ground, the only sound was the electronic crackle of malfunctioning sensors inside his helmet. His vision came back in a swarm of tiny, buzzing pixels, a landscape that eventually reformulated to become the face of the thing as it reared up and thundered toward him again.

At the last second, Mando rolled over, groaning. He raised his arm and blasted the creature's face with a jet of flame. It bellowed with rage but didn't retreat, even as the flame spluttered out. He fired his grappling wire at it, latched on, and too late realized his mistake. Now he was tethered to it, and the mudhorn whipped him furiously along behind it, the wire swinging him upward until it flung him back down again. He groped for his weapons, feeling nothing but empty space.

His rifle was gone. His blaster was gone. And with them, all remaining hope.

The mudhorn, seeming to sense the moment of triumph had arrived, turned around and lowered its head. It pounded its head against the ground, roared, and charged.

Reaching down, Mando drew his knife.

He held it in front of him with both hands. Maybe there was a vulnerable spot on the thing's neck, a blood vessel that he could slash or puncture, and he might stand a chance. If not, then at least he could leave this creature with a scar, something to remember him by.

He closed his eyes and waited.

And then nothing happened.

A moment later, he was aware of the thing bellowing again somewhere directly in front of him. But this time it sounded different—more of the bewildered honk of a predator that had encountered something utterly new and incomprehensible.

The Mandalorian looked up and frowned, not quite able to believe his eyes.

Immediately in front of him, close enough that he almost could have reached up and touched it, the mudhorn floated in midair. Its stumpy legs paddled helplessly above the ground as it bucked and snarled and swung its head from side to side, caught in an invisible web it didn't understand, its horn swishing through empty space.

Mando stood there, wondering if what he was seeing was a hallucination, the result of some kind of head injury or a malfunctioning visor. Nothing—literally *nothing*—about this made any sense. And yet there it was, and the longer he stared, the more convinced he was that it was real. But how . . . ?

Then he looked back at the Child.

The Child was right where he'd been all along, in the floating silver pram that had followed Mando out to the cave. But he was doing something Mando hadn't seen before.

The Child's eyes were closed, his features pinched in concentration, and one tiny hand was extended outward in the direction of the mudhorn. His entire body was trembling, practically quivering with the intensity of his efforts—straining as if he was using every drop of strength to lift some unimaginably great weight.

Mando realized that was exactly what was happening.

The moment lingered, until all at once the Child seemed to reach the limit of whatever it was he was doing. He fell backward into the pram while—at the same moment—the mudhorn dropped to the ground with a startled bray of confusion.

The Mandalorian saw his chance.

Launching forward, he swung his arm up and drove his blade into the thing's neck, pushing it to the hilt. The beast roared again, but it was already weakening, staggering, all the fight pouring out of it. With a final, defeated breath, it fell back, rolled onto its side, and sank into the mud, the knife protruding from its neck. Mando fell next to it, completely wrung out.

A moment later he forced himself to stand up, reached over, and plucked his blade loose, then made his way over to the silver pram. Inside, the Child lay motionless, eyes closed. He looked as drained as the Mandalorian felt. Gazing down at him, the bounty hunter was aware of the first of a thousand questions rising in his mind, questions that weren't going to have any easy answers.

But there wasn't time for that yet.

He turned and walked back toward the mouth of the cave.

When he returned to the sandcrawler with the Egg, the Jawas were already packing up to leave. The Mandalorian could see the loading ramp being retracted and knew that if he'd been any later, it all would've been for nothing. Kuiil was waiting, and when the Jawas saw Mando coming, they turned hopefully in his direction.

"I've got it," Mando said. "I've got the Egg."

When they realized what was in his hands, a great cheer went up among the Jawas, and they rushed toward him, surrounding him and taking it from him. The object in question was a large oval covered in a layer of slippery, mud-caked hair.

Mando watched as the Jawas carried their prize back toward the crawler, one of them taking it and holding it up with a cry of victory, displaying it to the others like a sacred artifact. A moment later, the Jawa leader pulled out a knife and hacked off the top of the egg to expose the bright yellow fluid within it. All the others pushed in close, dipping their hands in the stuff and pulling it out in thick, gooey strands, then shoving it delightedly into their mouths.

The Mandalorian looked at them and shook his head. He walked over to where Kuiil was standing. "I'm surprised you waited."

"I'm surprised you took so long," Kuiil said, and examined the Mandalorian's battered armor. "I assume there's another story to tell?"

"There is," the Mandalorian said.

They rode back to camp that night, Kuiil astride his blurrg, pulling the lev-loader, which was piled high with all the parts of the *Razor Crest* that the Jawas had returned. The Mandalorian sat in front with the Child, who was in his pram, eyes still closed.

"Is it still sleeping?" Kuiil asked.

"Yes."

"Was it injured?"

"I don't think so," Mando said. "Not physically."

"Explain it to me again," Kuiil said, reflecting back on

what the bounty hunter had told him. "I still don't understand what happened."

"Neither do I."

They rode on in silence, each lost in his own thoughts. Kuiil kept looking at the Child. He had never seen anything like it, and although he didn't doubt a word of what the Mandalorian had told him, it was still difficult to believe. Defeating a mudhorn was one thing. Making such a beast float in the air . . . especially done by a tiny creature such as this . . . He simply couldn't grasp it.

When they reached the *Razor Crest*, Kuiil watched as the Mandalorian climbed down and assessed his badly damaged ship, then shook his head in resignation.

"There's no way we're going to get this to work without a full maintenance facility," the bounty hunter said. "This is gonna take days to fix."

"If you care to help," Kuiil said, "it might go faster. There is much work to do."

They labored through the rest of the night, reinstalling the pieces the Jawas had ripped out, soldering the wires, and welding components into place. For Kuiil, it was an opportunity to lose himself in something he loved. He had always found deep satisfaction in repairing broken things, listening to what was wrong with a piece of machinery and coaxing it back to life. Occasionally he even caught himself speaking softly to the ship's onboard computers as he worked, like a doctor assuring a patient that everything was going to be fine.

Little by little, the *Crest* began to come back together. By morning, he and the Mandalorian were standing side by side in the cockpit. The bounty hunter activated the ship's main engines, looking out as the burners responded.

"I can't thank you enough," Mando said. "Please allow me to give you a portion of the reward."

Kuiil regarded him with an appreciative gaze. "I cannot accept," he said. "You are my guest, and I am therefore in your service."

The bounty hunter nodded, and then seemed to consider a different tact. "I could use a crew member of your ability," he said, "and I can pay handsomely."

"I am honored," Kuiil answered, "but I have worked a lifetime to finally be free of servitude."

Mando nodded again. "I understand. Then all I can offer is my thanks."

"And I offer mine," Kuiil told him. "Thank you for bringing peace to my valley."

They left the cockpit and made their way down the boarding ramp and out of the ship, where the Ugnaught's blurrg waited for him. Kuiil mounted it, then raised one arm to the bounty hunter in a salute. "And good luck with the Child. May it survive and bring you a handsome reward." He paused. "I have spoken."

CHAPTER

10

AS THE *RAZOR CREST* lifted off, the Mandalorian entered coordinates into the navicomputer and waited as the ship made its calculations for the long flight ahead. He grasped the throttle and eased it steadily forward.

He glanced back at the pram, and the tiny, motionless shape inside.

The Child still hadn't moved or opened his eyes. The effort of levitating the mudhorn had worn him out. Mando gave the pram a gentle shake, but nothing happened. Maybe the occupant was only sleeping. He returned his attention to the flight console.

From behind him, he heard a soft cooing sound.

Turning, he saw the Child was sitting upright, bright eyes open and gleaming, watching him with the same interest he'd shown earlier. The Mandalorian looked back at him.

The Child was alive and well, and for the moment that was enough.

The Mandalorian did a final check on their course to Nevarro and prepared for the long journey back.

Later, he heard the soft rustle of fabric, blankets being pushed aside, and realized that the Child had climbed out of his silver hover pram, had dropped to the floor, and was toddling toward Mando. Something on the ship's console had caught his eye, some small, shiny object.

Before Mando could see what it was, he heard a shrill beep, and the holoprojector came online to reveal the image of Greef Karga, standing with hands on hips, looking unmistakably pleased.

"Mando," he said. "I received your transmission. Wonderful news. Upon your return, deliver your quarry directly to the Client." The Guild agent chuckled. "I have no idea if he wants to eat it or hang it on his wall, but he's very antsy." Then, with a nod: "Safe passage. You know where to find me."

Mando glanced over at the Child, who was busy unscrewing the ball from one of the ship's control levers and holding it up in front of him, looking like he was going to put it in his mouth. The bounty hunter took it away. "That's not a toy," he said, and hoisted the Child by the back of his cloak, hearing a slight squeaking coo as he settled him in his hover pram and prepared to make the final approach to Nevarro.

Walking through the crowded streets amid the mingled smells and gray postindustrial grime of the city, the Mandalorian made his way back to the safe house where he'd agreed to meet the Client. He went down the alleyway, with the Child in the pram hovering along behind him, then stopped and pounded on the door.

Moments later, a sentry droid extended a long, telescoping stalk ending in a single red eye. The droid gibbered something, a combination of a question and a challenge.

Mando brought out the chit that Greef had given him at the beginning of the assignment and held it up so the red eye could see it, and a second later the door slid open. Inside stood a pair of renegade stormtroopers, blasters at the ready. The troopers stepped out, then glanced dismissively at the Child and back at Mando before taking hold of the pram and pulling it roughly inside.

"Easy with that," Mando said.

One stormtrooper glared at him. "You take it easy."

They went inside, down a narrow concourse, and through another pair of doors. Up ahead, in another, larger room, the Client was sitting behind a desk, with Dr. Pershing standing at his side. When the older man saw them come in, he rose to his feet, not bothering to disguise his excitement. "Yes," he said, approaching the pram and bending down to look at the Child. "Yes, yes, yes."

The Child whimpered softly as Pershing brought out a

sensor and waved it in front of his tiny face and shined it in his eyes, the amber light casting complex patterns as the device passed over his features.

"Very healthy," the doctor said. "*Yes.*"

The Client straightened up to look at the Mandalorian. "Your reputation was not unwarranted."

"How many fobs did you give out?" Mando asked, thinking of the IG bounty droid, and the Trandoshans who'd ambushed him back on Arvala-7, and whoever else might have tried to kill him during the course of the assignment.

"This asset was of extreme importance to me," the Client said, as if that were an answer, "and I had to ensure its delivery." Turning, he went back to his desk and picked up a large, cylindrical carrier. "But to the winner go the spoils." He tapped in the combination, and the carrier spread open like the petals of a metal flower to reveal a stack of beskar plates within.

The Mandalorian walked over and reached down to pick up one of the plates, hefting the unmistakable weight in his hand. He was aware of the Client watching him as he did so.

"Such a large bounty for such a small package," the old man said.

Off to his right, Mando heard the sound of crying. He looked over and watched as Pershing began to push the pram out of the room. Mando could see the Child turning to look back at him, clearly not understanding what was happening, his expression increasingly fearful and confused. Then they passed through another doorway and were gone.

The door closed behind them.

The bounty hunter looked up at the Client. "What are your plans for it?"

The old man raised an eyebrow, seemingly amused by the question. "How uncharacteristic of one of your reputation. You have taken both commission and payment. Is it not the code of the Guild that these events are now forgotten?"

The Mandalorian said nothing. He was aware of another door whooshing open behind the old man and two additional stormtroopers coming in, their presence emphasizing the fact that his business there was complete and it was time for him to move on.

"That beskar is enough to make a handsome replacement for your armor," the Client continued. "Unfortunately, finding a Mandalorian in these trying times is more difficult than finding the steel."

Mando looked at him for a long moment, at the troopers, and down at the beskar. Then he reached for the container, sealed it, and picked it up. The metal *was* surprisingly heavy, and its weight dragged on him like an anchor as he turned and carried it out the door.

"This amount can be shaped many ways," the Armorer said.

Mando gazed across the forge at her, the two of them

seated in the shadows cast by the blue fire. "My armor has lost its integrity," he said. "I may need to begin again."

"Indeed. I can form a full breastplate," she said, and then added: "I must warn you, it may draw many eyes."

From behind the Mandalorian, as if to illustrate the Armorer's statement, came the sound of footsteps, followed by a scoffing grunt of disapproval. A large Mandalorian male named Paz Vizsla was standing there. "These were cast in an Imperial smelter," Vizsla said. "These are the spoils of the Great Purge. The reason we live hidden like sand rats."

"Our secrecy is our survival," the Armorer said. "Our survival is our strength."

"Our strength was once in our numbers," the other soldier said. "Now we live in the shadows and only come above ground one at a time." As the man spoke, the anger in his voice grew steadily sharper and more intense. "Our world was shattered by the Empire, with whom *this* coward"—he indicated Mando—"shares tables."

When the hand landed on Mando's arm, he sprang up to meet his challenger, blade at the ready. Vizsla swung at him, his own knife coming to rest under Mando's helmet. The two of them gazed at each other, neither one moving, each waiting to see what the other would do.

The Armorer stood up. "The Empire is no longer," she said. "And the beskar has returned. When one chooses to walk the way of the Mandalore, you are both hunter and prey.

How can one be a coward if one chooses this way of life?" She turned to Mando. "Have you ever removed your helmet?"

"No," he said.

"Has it ever been removed by others?"

"Never."

She nodded. "This is the Way," and the others repeated it together, bringing a kind of unity between them, exactly as she'd intended.

Mando took a step back from the infantryman and felt some of the tension easing from the room. "This is the Way," he said.

The Armorer turned her attention to the fractured breastplate and shoulder piece of his armor. "What caused this damage?"

"A mudhorn."

"Then you have earned the mudhorn as your signet," she said. "I shall craft it."

"I can't accept," Mando said. "It wasn't a noble kill." He hesitated. "I was helped by an enemy."

"Why would an enemy help you in battle?"

He thought of the Child holding up his hand, the strain of the effort making him tremble. "It . . . did not know it was my enemy."

"Since you forgo a signet, I shall use the excess to forge whistling birds," the Armorer said, referring to a Mandalorian weapon. "They are a powerful defense against enemies. Use them sparingly, for they are rare."

The Mandalorian stepped back to wait. As the Armorer worked the metal in the forge, something about the crash of the hammer and the hiss of molten steel summoned memories with merciless clarity—sounds and sensations so vivid that they didn't seem like memories at all but the events themselves happening all over again.

There he was with his parents, the three of them terribly exposed and hunted across open ground as the street exploded around them, the battle droids closing in. Mando could smell the smoke and hear the screams. He saw his parents' faces as the world closed in around them. He felt his mother's hands press against his shoulders, holding him tightly one last time before they placed him in a bunker, closing the doors. The final glimpse of them was reduced to a thin sliver of light before an explosion wiped away all trace that they'd ever existed—

Mando caught his breath. His heart was pounding, his throat dry as the sand of Arvala-7. He'd seen it all again—*lived* it again. It wasn't the first time, nor would it be the last.

CHAPTER

11

"I WANT MY NEXT JOB."

Mando and Greef Karga were at the public house, seated at Karga's regular table. The Mandalorian had walked in wearing his newly forged armor, made from freshly shaped beskar that still gleamed from the Armorer's forge. The helmet and visor had kicked back glints of light as he made his way across the room.

As he'd sat down, there was no mistaking the jealousy and resentment in the eyes of the other hunters around them, all of whom had no doubt seen the Client's reward as rightfully their own. Karga, who was delighted to raise his glass to his most famous hunter's success, and the fortune it had brought them both, had tapped the plate of beskar he'd tucked away in his front pocket, over his heart.

"Even *I'm* rich." Karga had chuckled, and then appeared disappointed that his companion didn't join him in his glee. He might not have expected the bounty hunter to gloat over his victory, but the Mandalorian's immediate request for more work had clearly caught him off guard.

"Next *job*?" Karga's face seemed to grow longer with disbelief. "Why don't you take some time off? Enjoy yourself."

"I want my next job."

Karga sighed. "Fine," he said. "I know you hunters like to stay busy."

The Mandalorian waited. Before their conversation was over, he had accepted the highest paying bounty that Karga had to offer, a nobleman's son who had skipped bail. With the bounty puck in his hand, he got up and walked out, determined to get to his ship and leave Nevarro as soon as possible . . . as if that would somehow erase the memory of the Child.

And at first it actually did seem to help.

A new mission, the new armor, the familiar rituals of boarding the *Razor Crest*, powering up the engines, and entering in the destination coordinates for the navigation system . . . all of these things were enough to take his mind off what he was leaving behind.

He almost made it.

But then he reached for the lever.

That was where the ball had been, the one that the Child had unscrewed because it was small and bright and round, and caught his eye. The Mandalorian looked down. The ball itself was lying next to the lever.

He picked it up and rolled it between his fingers, thinking again of the Child's frightened face as Dr. Pershing had pushed the pram away, remembering that fearful, plaintive cry. As he reattached the ball, screwing it back into place, he paused, lost in thought.

He powered the engines down, climbed out of the ship, and started back to town.

"*I don't care,*" the Client was saying, his voice crackling from the long-distance microphone Mando held to the earpiece inside his helmet. "*I order you to extract the necessary material and be done with it.*"

Mando was perched on a rooftop using the scanner in his helmet to listen in on the conversation. He'd crept up there after emerging from the alleyway alongside the safe house, where he had found the Child's hover pram shoved into a refuse bin. Seeing it there, tossed out like common trash, eliminated any remaining doubt he might have had about what he'd come back to do.

He walked up to the entrance to the safe house, placed the thermal detonator against the door, and set the timing device. What happened next would either succeed or fail, but he already knew there was no other choice.

From that point on, there would be no turning back.

In the years to come, when the balladeers of Nevarro spoke of the day the Mandalorian broke the Code and signed his own death warrant, there were as many different versions of the events as there were ears to hear it.

But it always started with the explosion.

The gray charge was powerful enough to rip the door from its gaskets, and a moment later Mando was inside the safe house, making his way through the smoke and flying sparks, already taking fire from the stormtroopers (some said a dozen, some said more) who'd come running at the sound. The troopers did what they were famous for—fighting, then dying—while Mando fought his way back through the tunnel leading to Dr. Pershing's lab.

When he walked in, Pershing was already in the process of extracting something from the Child. Mando grabbed the doctor and thrust him aside, and Pershing landed on the floor, on his knees, hands held up in front of his face.

"Please!" he said "I'm trying to save it! I'm the only reason it's still alive!"

Mando picked up the Child and tucked it under his arm. Turning, he stepped back out into the corridor, blaster at the ready.

The stormtroopers were already swarming toward him, firing from all sides. Dodging, the bounty hunter drew back, fired, and disappeared into the shadows. He could hear more troopers running down through the adjoining corridor, conferring with one another, determined to flush him out. A volley of blaster fire tore through the hallway. A shot struck the wall beside his head, and he felt the Child flinch in his arms.

The Mandalorian fired back, then turned and saw a trooper in front of him preparing to shoot. He pointed the prongs at the end of his disruptor rifle at the attacker's breastplate and sent a crackling burst of electricity through his armor. Aiming at the second trooper, behind him, the bounty hunter blasted him with his flamethrower and sent him backward, howling.

Still they kept coming. At the end of the hallway, he cut back the way he'd entered, pausing to listen to the footsteps of more troopers, then taking them out. By the time he'd reached the Client's office, where he'd first accepted the beskar, he found himself surrounded.

"Freeze!"

"Don't move!"

"Hands up!"

"Drop the blaster!"

The Mandalorian felt the weight of the Child in his arms, heard him whimper, saw the gleaming eyes moving to look up at him. Slowly, he lowered his weapon.

"Wait," he said. "What I'm holding is very valuable. Here . . ."

He knelt down and placed his blaster pistol on the floor in front of him, and as the stormtroopers came in closer . . .

Whistling birds.

The tiny projectiles burst out of his gauntlet, spiraling and corkscrewing in a dozen different directions at once, cutting through the troopers with lethal precision. Within seconds, they had all dropped to the floor.

Mando stepped over their bodies and kept moving.

All across Nevarro, in every cantina and on every street corner, every bounty hunter's fob began blinking red.

Emerging from the safe house and into the open, the Mandalorian didn't need to look around to sense the net closing around him. He recognized the footsteps of his competitors, heard the high-pitched electronic alerts going off, pinging off the walls of the city. The atmosphere seemed to constrict around him, as if the air itself was a web. At the far end of the street, he saw Greef Karga waiting for him, his old friend's hands spread in a gesture of false pleasantry.

"Welcome back, Mando!" Karga exclaimed, and then, with all his pretense draining away: "Now put the package down."

The Mandalorian didn't move. "Step aside," he said, aware of the sheer scope of firepower pointed in his direction from all sides. No one moved. To his right, perhaps a meter away, there was a slight humming sound coming from a commercial speeder piloted by a frightened-looking R6 unit. "I'm going to my ship."

"You put the bounty down," Karga said, "and perhaps I'll let you pass."

"The kid's coming with me."

"If you truly care about the kid," Karga replied, "then you'll put it on the speeder, and we'll discuss terms."

This was the standard back-and-forth, and Mando knew what his next question was expected to be. "How do I know I can trust you?"

"Because I'm your only hope," Karga replied, with the utter confidence of someone who completely believed every word he was saying.

It seemed that Greef Karga had flattered himself into believing that he knew Mando, and could predict what the Mandalorian would do, what he would choose, and how he would react. The Mandalorian looked at Karga and waited, letting the moment draw out.

Then, in a single, fluid motion, he leapt into the speeder, flipping his body to protect the Child, and started firing, taking out two of the nearest bounty hunters in the time that it took to land on the speeder's inside deck. The element of surprise was just enough for him to get the attention of the speeder droid.

"Drive!" Mando told it, and when the droid beeped a panicked refusal, he pointed his blaster at it. *"Drive!"*

The droid whooped, and the speeder burst into motion, careening down the street while Mando kept shooting, keeping the Child close to him, taking out hunters on either side—then switching over to the disruptor rifle to obliterate those last few before they could get in a shot. Somewhere Karga was roaring at them, somewhat absurdly, not to shoot the target. Everyone seemed to be shooting everywhere. At the far end of the street, the speeder finally collided with a pile of rubble, jerking to a halt, and from inside, Mando heard its thrusters die with a final hiss.

He raised his head, rifle at the ready. He saw Karga, the man very close to him, flanked by more hunters, nodding at the disruptor with genuine appreciation.

"That's one impressive weapon," the Guild agent said.

Mando didn't answer. He felt the Child stirring again in his arms. The adrenaline spike that had gotten him this far had begun to ebb. He'd taken the element of surprise as far as he could, and what would happen next was anyone's guess.

"Here's what I'm gonna do," Mando said. "I'm gonna walk to my ship with the kid, and you're going to let it happen."

"No," Karga said, "how about this. We take the kid, and if you try to stop us, we kill you and we strip your body for parts." This time, there was no sense of expectation in Karga's voice, no hint of trust or confidence. He was prepared to shoot, as were all the other hunters surrounding him.

Cornered, the balladeers of Nevarro would say, when

they spoke of it, the Mandalorian saw no way out. All that he had fought for, risked his life for, was about to come to an end as a consequence of his foolish defiance, the recklessness of his sin—

The next explosion, when it struck, came from above.

Mando looked up, as startled as everyone else to see heavily armored figures flying over the rooftops of the city. His eyes widened as he recognized who they were.

His fellow Mandalorians, their jet packs carrying them over the mob below, fired down at the hunters, sending them scattering. As they descended, Mando recognized Paz Vizsla, the Mandalorian soldier who'd challenged and confronted him at knifepoint by the Armorer's forge. Vizsla and several others had set up a tightly organized fire team that was forcing the bounty hunters backward, creating a pathway of escape.

"Get out of here!" he told Mando, shouting to be heard over the roar of heavy blaster fire. "We'll hold them off!"

"You're going to have to relocate," Mando said.

The soldier responded without hesitating. "This is the Way."

"This is the Way," Mando repeated.

He cradled the tiny, cowering form of the Child, turned in the direction of the ship, and began to run.

"Hold it, Mando," Karga said.

The Mandalorian was halfway up the ramp of the *Razor Crest* and turned to see the Guild agent standing there, brow furrowed, blaster in hand.

"I didn't want it to come to this," Karga said, "but then you broke the Code!"

Mando just looked at him. Incredibly, the man at the other end of the ramp actually seemed offended, as if what the Mandalorian had done were some sort of personal affront. Was it possible that, after everything that had happened—after threatening to kill him and strip him for parts—Greef Karga still somehow thought of Mando as a friend?

Hardly shifting his gaze away from Karga, he moved his arm and fired a cable bolt into the control panel, releasing a sudden cloud of pressurized gas that immediately filled the space between them. The cloud left Karga scowling and squinting, shifting his blaster erratically from side to side, trying to see where the Mandalorian was.

Then Mando shot him.

It wasn't until they were inside the cockpit of the *Razor Crest* and airborne, rising over Nevarro's atmosphere, that the bounty hunter reached over and unscrewed the ball from the top of the lever. He handed it back to the Child and felt the small, curious being take it from him with a soft coo of interest.

Mando looked at the Child's face and saw those big eyes gazing back at him. All that was left for them was to find somewhere to hide out—some backwater planet where they could wait for the heat to cool down.

Surely, such a place—a place of peace—would not be hard to find.

CHAPTER

12

THE VILLAGERS WERE still fishing when the raiders attacked.

Omera and the others had spent the morning with their nets, gathering great harvests of blue krill from the shallows, just as their parents and grandparents had done when they had first seeded those waters. Droids moved among them, carrying bags of the harvest. It was a good catch, Omera thought, and would feed the village well.

She looked up from her work and gazed across the green-and-blue landscape and the surrounding trees. Children were running, kicking a ball, laughing and playing games. Her daughter, Winta, was somewhere out there among them. Omera knew the time would come when her daughter would join them in their work with nets and wicker baskets. Then she saw her daughter chasing a frog along the creek and smiled.

Let her be a child, she thought, *for a little while longer. And later, perhaps—*

Her smile faded.

She could hear them coming.

Her breath froze in her lungs. There was a sound like thunder, the reverberation sending flocks of startled birds up from the branches. An instant later, the entire forest seemed to erupt—terrible red blaster fire smashing down from the upper limbs and exploding through the open land, blowing it to pieces and driving up plumes of smoke and water. With a sudden cry of terror, the villagers dropped their nets and fled.

"Mama!" Winta screamed, her voice bright with terror.

Omera saw her down in the creek where she'd been chasing the frog, and ran for her. Another blast from the cannons struck very close, shooting up a spray of water and steam, seeming to shake the very planet, and Winta screamed again.

Omera grabbed her daughter and pulled her down into the pond, holding her so just her head was above the surface. Beneath the water, she could feel Winta clutching her tightly, her small body trembling with fear. They were both breathless, wide-eyed, unable to speak.

They're coming, Omera thought.

Hardly thinking, she reached for one of the curved wicker baskets and flipped it upside down to cover their faces. She and her daughter peered out through the basket and saw the raiding party emerging out of the smoke.

The Klatooinian raiders charged into the village. They came as they always had in the past, with their weapons raised, roaring, ready to take what was not theirs. From where she and her daughter huddled in the water, Omera watched as the bandits poured into the camp, grabbing nets and bags and baskets, stealing the village's harvest, delighting in destruction. Omera stared as one of the raiders drove his spear into a droid, impaling its neural processor.

Finally, the raiders turned and carried off what they'd stolen, leaving the village burning in their wake. Omera held her daughter but couldn't bring herself to move.

She wondered if they would ever feel safe again.

The *Razor Crest* moved through space.

In the cockpit, the Mandalorian was focused on their next destination. The Child sat beside him, fascinated by the array of different-colored lights. He reached out and pushed one of the green buttons on the navigation console. *Click!* The ship's engines began making a slightly different sound. The Child cooed, happy with the outcome, and pushed another button—a red one this time. *Click!*

"Stop touching things," the Mandalorian said.

The Child looked at him, wide-eyed, not moving. Then,

very slowly, without looking away from Mando, he leaned over and pushed another button. *Click!* The ship started rattling and shaking, briefly veering off course.

Mando picked up the Child and moved him away from the controls. "Let's see," he said, checking the charts. "Sorgan. Looks like there's no starport, no industrial centers, no population density. Real backwater skug hole. Which means it's perfect for us." He glanced at the Child. "You ready to lay low and stretch your legs for a couple months, you little womp rat? Nobody's gonna find us here."

Nestled in his arms, the Child blinked and looked around, more interested in the red and green lights.

Carasynthia Dune had learned long before to sit with her back to the wall. It was the safest place to be.

From her usual table in the common house, she saw the Mandalorian walk in and take a seat. He wasn't traveling alone. Tottering along behind him was a small, childlike being with green skin, long ears, and big eyes. Cara watched as the Mandalorian lifted the being into a seat and settled in across from it, ordering a bowl of bone broth from the proprietor.

What are you doing here? Cara wondered.

Such vigilance was second nature to her, honed over years of survival in dangerous and sometimes deadly circumstances. During the war, she had served the Rebel Alliance as a shock trooper, going in where the action was hot, infiltrating areas that traditional infantry couldn't, fighting her way out without support. She'd learned to trust her instincts, and those instincts had kept her alive.

And right then, they were telling her it was time to go.

She stood up and slipped out the door and around the corner, hurried down the enclosed space between buildings, then waited in the shadows, listening.

A moment later, the Mandalorian followed. Cara heard him coming and waited until he was close enough to attack. She leapt up to grab an overhanging bar, swinging her feet forward to kick him in the chest. While he was still recovering, she landed and punched him hard in the head and again in the torso, knocking him back against the wall. He lunged forward, swinging, and hit her in the ribs, then smashed her in the face. Cara grabbed him by the throat, underneath his helmet, and hurled him down with a grunt.

The bounty hunter activated his flamethrower. Cara launched herself into the air and brought both feet down on top of him as hard as she could. Swinging herself around, she grabbed her blaster, and they ended up on the ground, both of them panting for breath, weapons pointed at each other's faces.

Off to the side, Cara heard slurping sounds. She looked over and saw the child the Mandalorian had brought with him, watching them while happily sipping from a bowl of bone broth.

"You want some soup?" the Mandalorian asked.

Back in the common house, they sat down at the table and Cara told him what she'd been up to. "Saw most of my action mopping up after Endor," she said. "Mostly ex-Imperial warlords. They wanted it fast and quiet. They'd send us in on the drop ships. Then when the Imperials were gone, the politics started." She shook her head. "Not what I signed up for."

"How'd you end up here?" the Mandalorian asked.

"Let's just call it an early retirement." She took a sip from her bowl and looked at him. "Look, I knew you were in the Guild. I figured you had a fob on me. That's why I came at you so hard."

"Yeah, that's what I figured," Mando said.

She stood up. "Well, this has been a real treat, but unless you wanna go another round, one of us is gonna have to move on, and I was here first."

As she walked away, the Mandalorian looked at the Child, who gave him a quizzical glance. "Looks like this planet's taken," he said. "We'll leave in the morning."

That night, as he was preparing the *Razor Crest* for an early-morning departure, he heard someone making their way through the trees. If it was an enemy, they were doing a terrible job of sneaking up on him. A moment later, two men stepped out of the woods, one young, one slightly older, neither looking too sure of himself.

"Excuse me," one of them said, sounding nervous. "Excuse me, sir?"

Mando turned. "Is there something I can help you with?"

They hesitated, and then the first one spoke up again. "Raiders, sir."

"We have money," the other added.

The bounty hunter regarded them for a moment. Both men were staring at him with a mixture of hope and desperation. "So you think I'm some kind of mercenary?"

"You *are* a Mandalorian, right? Or at least wearing Mandalorian armor?" The younger of the two men was almost breathless with excitement. "Sir, I've read a lot about your people . . . your tribe . . . and if half of what I've read is true—"

"We have money," the other repeated, holding up a bag to show him.

"How much?" Mando asked.

"It's everything we have, sir." He swallowed hard, the muscles in this throat tightening. "Our whole harvest was stolen."

"Krill," the other man added. "We're krill farmers."

"We brew spotchka. Our whole village chipped in."

The Mandalorian looked at the small sack of credits in

the man's trembling hand. "It's not enough," he said, and turned away.

"Are you sure? You don't even know what the job is!"

"I know it's not enough," Mando said. "Good luck." Before they could respond, he hit the switch to extend the boarding ramp of the *Crest*, which expelled a sudden gust of steam as it lowered. The two men drew back, muttering to themselves over the failure of their mission.

"It took us a whole day to get here," the younger one complained. "Now we have to ride back in the dark, with no protection, to the middle of nowhere. . . ."

Mando raised his head. "Where do you live?"

"On a farm," the man who'd brought the bag of money said, looking over his shoulder. "Weren't you listening? We're farmers."

He thought again about the promise of sanctuary, a place where he and the Child might be safe, an opportunity to regroup and decide on his next move. Perhaps this planet might work out after all, at least for a while. "In the middle of nowhere?"

The older one nodded. "Yes."

"You have lodging?"

"Yeah," the younger man said, "absolutely."

"Good," Mando said. "Come up and help."

The two exchanged puzzled glances, not sure exactly why their luck had suddenly changed, and then set to work.

As they helped load supplies in the lifter, preparing to head out for their village, the bounty hunter realized someone else might be able to help.

"I'm going to need one more thing," he said, and held out his hand. "Give me those credits."

The older man looked at him in surprise. "So now it *is* going to be enough?"

Mando put the last of the bags on the lifter. "We'll see," he said.

He found Cara Dune sitting by her campfire, eyes alert, blaster already pointed at him. Mando responded by tossing the bag of credits at her feet.

"Ready for round two?" he asked.

She frowned, but lowered her blaster to listen. The credits bought him enough time to explain the situation that the two men from the village had presented him. Based on the information they'd provided, he thought he could use another pair of hands, someone who knew their way around a blaster.

"So we're basically running off a band of raiders for lunch money?" Cara asked when he'd finished describing the situation.

"They're quartering us in the middle of nowhere," Mando said. "Last I checked, it's a pretty square deal for somebody in your position. Worst-case scenario, you tune up your blaster. Best case, we're a deterrent." He turned to regard the woods around them. "I can't imagine there's anything living in these trees that an ex-shock trooper couldn't handle."

Cara said nothing, just gazed at the fire. The Mandalorian leaned back and waited for her decision. He already had a feeling what she was going to say.

CHAPTER

13

BY DAWN the next morning their speeder had emerged from the woods, gliding into the village. News of their arrival must have reached the villagers already, since a group of local children rushed out to meet the speeder. Mando and Cara watched as the kids came running up, laughing and waving, taking an immediate interest in the Child, who looked back at them, his hands raised, cooing with pleasure.

"Looks like they're happy to see us," the Mandalorian said.

Cara's expression remained neutral. "Looks like."

He climbed out of the back of the speeder and began to unload the supplies. From what he could see, the village itself was a cluster of huts and barns with thatched roofs, surrounded by a series of small ponds with nets suspended above them, where the villagers and farmers caught their krill. A peaceful community of fish farmers where nothing could be terribly threatening.

Walking through the camp, Mando carried his gear over to the barn where he was told he would be staying. The woman inside was drawing the blinds from the window to let in the light. She had dark hair and kind, welcoming eyes. She smiled at him. "Please come in," she said. "My name is Omera. I hope this is comfortable for you. I'm sorry that all we have is the barn."

"This will do fine," Mando said, and set down the case he'd brought with him.

"I stacked some blankets over here."

"Thank you. That's very kind—" Something moved in the corner of his eye, and he spun around on reflex, blaster already in his hand. Looking toward the doorway, he saw a small girl cowering just outside. He lowered his weapon, but the fright remained in her eyes as she went to the woman's side.

"This is my daughter, Winta," Omera said. "We don't get a lot of visitors around here. She's not used to strangers." She ran her hand over the girl's head reassuringly. "This nice man is going to help protect us from the bad ones."

The girl looked at him. "Thank you."

"Come on, Winta," Omera said. "Let's give our guests some room."

Later the two of them returned, just as he'd begun

cleaning his rifle. This time Omera brought a tray with food, and Winta glanced at the Child, who was perched in a makeshift crib next to Mando's bunk, blinking up at the visitors with bright-eyed interest.

"Can I feed him?" Winta asked.

"Sure."

The girl knelt down. "Are you hungry?" she asked, and giggled when the Child accepted the morsel of food she'd held out for him. She looked back at Mando. "Can I play with him?"

He sighed. "Sure." Lifting the Child from the crib, he set him down on the hardwood floor.

"Come on!" Winta said, and ran out, the Child gurgling happily as he started to follow.

"I don't think—" Mando began.

"They'll be fine," Omera said.

"I don't—"

"They'll be fine." Omera smiled at him again, and he felt some of his misgivings starting to dissolve. "I brought you some food," she said. "I notice you didn't eat out there. I'll leave it here for you when I go."

"That's very thoughtful of you," he said, turning back to his task, but she was still standing in the doorway looking at him.

"Do you mind if I ask you something?"

The bounty hunter nodded. "Go ahead."

"How long has it been since you've taken that off?"

"My helmet?" He paused. "Yesterday."

"I mean in front of someone else."

Mando glanced out at where the children were playing, with the Child toddling happily alongside, making small noises of excitement. "I wasn't much older than they are," he said.

"You haven't shown your face to anyone since you were a kid?"

"No," he said. "I was happy that they took me in. My parents were killed and the Mandalorians took care of me."

"I'm sorry," she said softly.

He looked back at her. "This is the Way."

Omera gazed at him again for a moment. "Let us know if there's anything you need."

"Thank you," he said, and stood watching as she turned to go. After she was gone, he sat down at the table where she'd placed the food. Through the window he could hear the children playing outside, laughing and running in circles. Their voices sounded happy, carefree, full of life. The Child was among them, giggling, too, perfectly in his element.

Mando reached up to grasp his helmet, lifted it off, and began to eat.

That evening, Mando and Cara walked the area surrounding the village. It was a good night for a reconnaissance mission.

The twilight was peaceful, the air virtually silent except for the faint chirring of insects. Reaching up, Mando made an adjustment on his visor, and the infrared scope switched on to reveal a series of footprints leading into the forest.

"About fifteen or twenty of them came through here on foot," he said, and gestured toward the trees ahead. "And something big sheared off those branches." They went a little farther and stopped again, neither of them speaking as they squatted down next to an enormous print in the soft dirt.

"AT-ST," Cara said.

"Imperial walker." Mando was still examining it. "What's it doing out here?"

"I don't know," she said as they stood up. "But this is more than I signed up for."

He agreed. What the villagers had initially described had sounded like a standard gang of thieves, nothing out of the ordinary. But this was different. Since the fall of the Empire, there had been countless reports of stolen military supplies, weapons, and transports being sold on the black market and scattered across the galaxy. With enough credits, you could buy whatever you wanted.

"There's only one way out of this," she said, "as far as I can see. And they're not going to like it."

"Bad news," Mando said. "You can't live here anymore."

The villagers gathered in front of the barn murmured in

disbelief and confusion. Up in front, Omera and Winta were standing next to each other with matching expressions of uncertainty and concern.

Cara raised an eyebrow at the Mandalorian. "Nice bedside manner."

"You think you can do better?"

"Can't do much worse." She stepped forward, spreading her hands in a gesture of sympathy. "Look, I know this isn't the news you wanted to hear," she told the villagers. "But there are no other options."

"You took the job," someone protested, and Mando saw that the speaker was one of the men who had approached his ship with the bag of credits.

"That was before we knew about the AT-ST," Cara said.

She might as well have switched over to another language. The entire crowd looked totally bewildered.

"What's that?" someone said.

"The armored walker with two enormous guns that you knew about and didn't tell us," Cara said. If she'd expected this to somehow convince the villagers, it had exactly the opposite result. Now everyone was pleading with them to stay and fight. The Mandalorian saw Omera looking at them, her daughter still at her side.

"We have no other place to go," Omera said.

"Sure you do," Cara said. "This is a big planet. I mean, I've seen a lot smaller."

The crowd wouldn't be convinced. "My grandparents seeded these ponds," one of the farmers said. "It took generations to develop what we have here."

"I understand," Cara said. "I do. But there are only two of us."

"No, there's not. There's at least twenty here!"

"I mean *fighters*," Cara told them. "Be realistic." Her tone darkened. "I've seen that thing take out entire companies of soldiers in a matter of minutes."

For a moment the villagers murmured among themselves, and in the midst of it, Mando heard Omera's voice above the others, not loud but still strong enough to command attention.

"We're not leaving," Omera said.

Cara met her gaze. "You cannot fight that thing."

The bounty hunter found himself looking at the young woman who had welcomed him into their village, providing food and shelter. Her expression hadn't changed. It was the face of a survivor refusing to give in to fear, determined to stand her ground, whatever the cost.

Mando turned to Cara. "Unless we show them how," he said.

CHAPTER

14

STANDING AT THE EDGE of a clearing, Mando and Cara outlined the plan for the villagers. "You've got two problems here," he said. "The bandits and the mech. We'll handle the AT-ST, but you've got to protect us when they come out of the woods."

The group stood, listening attentively. Now that he and Cara had agreed to help them, the villagers were ready to do whatever was necessary to defend themselves—most of them, anyway. In the back, Mando recognized the faces of Stoke and Caben, the two men who'd initially offered him credits to fight for them, looking decidedly uncertain of their own ability to fight.

"How are we supposed to take down an Imperial walker?" Caben asked.

"Good question," Cara said, and stepped forward. "There's nothing on this planet that can damage the legs on this thing," she said. "So we're gonna build a trap." She gestured to the swampland behind her, where the ground gave way to a series of ponds. "We're going to dig real deep, right here. And when that thing steps in, it drops."

"I need you to cut down trees to build barricades along these edges," Mando said. "I need it high enough so that they can't get over, and strong enough that it can't break through." He surveyed the faces in front of him and got to the big question, the one he'd been building up to. "Okay, who knows how to shoot?"

Silence. Nobody moved.

Then Omera raised her hand.

She wasn't lying. At target practice, while the rest of the group potted away with varying degrees of accuracy at a row of pans and skillets hanging from a branch, Omera shot with confidence and precision, hitting her mark every time.

In the distance he could hear Cara Dune working with the others, training them on basic hand-to-hand combat maneuvers using the sharpened spears and pikes they'd made. They sounded determined, if nothing else, and that was good. In the end, when nightfall came they'd need every advantage they had, and the battle might come down to sheer willpower.

As dusk approached, Omera found Mando in the barn, making last-minute preparations. "We'll be leaving soon," he said. "When we return, we're coming in hot."

She nodded. "We'll be ready."

Mando looked at her, saying nothing.

"Let's go," Cara said, outside the barn, and he turned to leave.

The woods were almost completely dark, the night sky moonless, providing perfect cover for the operation. Mando and Cara made their way forward, their footsteps muffled by the layer of dried leaves and tree needles underfoot. Gradually they began to hear the indistinct grunts and voices of two raiders beside a perimeter bonfire in the distance.

Klatooinians.

They were humanoid, with greenish-brown skin, imposing brows, and toothy, snarling underbites that made them look especially vicious. The ones by the fire were eating and drinking—mainly drinking, from the sound of clinking cups of blue spotchka being gulped down and their increasingly slurred words. Their recent successes in the village had left them bullish and overconfident, and they'd made no effort to stay vigilant.

He and Cara stepped into the firelight. Both guards looked up, utterly startled. One dropped his cup and started to stand, but he never made it to his feet before Cara hit him, doubling him over and finishing him off with a punch to the head. Mando took the other out, and a moment later, they were moving again, heads down, running farther into the camp.

Up ahead was the main encampment, an outpost of solid buildings with some sort of blue light trickling from inside. The Mandalorian glanced at Cara, and she nodded. This was the place.

Lifting the tent's flap, they slipped inside.

The tent appeared to be deserted. All around them, large circular tanks filled with blue spotchka cast watery shadows around the inside of the canvas, giving the space an ethereal, haunted look. Mando took out a gray charge, switched it on, and attached the blinking red device to one of the walls. Outside he could hear voices, talking and laughing, as more raiders drew near. Then, abruptly, the voices fell silent.

He glanced at Cara, saw that she understood what was happening, and the tent flaps opened again.

The bandits came bursting in with a roar of fury. Mando and Cara took them out with a combination of punches and kicks. One unlucky raider ended up with his head shoved into a bubbling pool of blue spotchka. But when the second wave arrived, someone started blasting, and Mando saw he and Cara were penned in. Getting out was going to be harder than he'd anticipated. Meanwhile the detonator's timing device had sped up to an almost panicky *beep-beep-beep-beep*.

He turned, drew his blaster, and opened fire on the opposite wall, blowing it apart until it was weak enough for Cara Dune to smash through. "Go, I'll cover you!" he told her. A moment later, he followed her through the hole in the wall and the entire operation erupted in a fireball behind them, big enough to throw them both to the ground and ignite the whole outpost.

Cara sat up, spitting dirt, and looked over at him. "I hope the plan worked," she said, and then they saw the pair of red eyes rising from the tree line until it towered over them with a grinding mechanical roar.

The run back to the village was a blur. Charging through the woods, the Mandalorian was aware of the walker immediately behind them. He heard and felt the heavy thunder of its feet and its cannons blasting dirt into the air on either side of them. The trench was up there somewhere, he knew, with the barricade behind it, a landscape dotted with orange flames from dozens of torches.

He and Cara ran across the narrow walkway that the villagers had built over the trench. Among the flickering torches, villagers waited, blasters and homemade weapons at the ready. They stared back at the forest. *"It's coming!"* someone whispered, and a surge of adrenaline passed through the line like an electric current.

Trees crashed, branches splintering, as the reddish portals of the AT-ST's control deck emerged from the forest, the thing stepping fully into view. From there it looked even bigger as it marched its way forward on bent, stork-like legs.

That's right, Mando thought. *Keep coming.* Mentally, he

measured the remaining distance as it stalked closer—twenty meters. He could feel his body tensing in anticipation. It took another step, and another.

Fifteen meters. Ten . . . five . . .

The walker stopped.

He scowled, sensing Cara's similar reaction alongside him. *What's it doing?*

A bright light from the walker snapped on, the beam sweeping the terrain in front of it, throwing long shadows across the shimmering expanse of ponds and huts. It swung across the barricade, and then behind it to the line of faces.

"Get down!" Mando hissed. "Get down!"

All at once, the thing started firing again, the cannons deafening. Cara looked back at the villagers. "Stay there!" she shouted. "Hold your positions!"

That was when he heard it coming out of the woods—a battle cry. An instant later, the Klatooinian raiding party burst forward, yelling and whooping, spilling toward the barricade with weapons held up.

"*Open fire!*" Cara yelled.

All at once, the landscape came alive with blaster bolts flying back and forth. Villagers rose up, firing on the bandits as they charged. The Mandalorian aimed at the walker's control cabin, but the thing's reinforced armor deflected the shots so they bounced harmlessly off its outer shell. It still hadn't budged from its place on the edge of the trench, and it didn't need to—from there, its twin blaster cannons rained down havoc on the village. The situation was deteriorating rapidly. From where he crouched, Mando could hear screaming as the people he'd agreed to protect found themselves helplessly outgunned, and it wouldn't be long before the walker finished the job.

He glanced at Cara. "We gotta get that thing to step forward!"

"I'm thinking," she said. "Give me the pulse rifle!"

"I'll cover you." He handed it to her, and she jumped up from behind the barricade, running hard for the trench, drawing the walker's fire. He got one last glimpse of her as she leapt into the trench and disappeared.

Come on, Cara, he thought. *You got this.*

The walker took another step, close enough that the tips of its feet were curling over the edge of the trench. Then abruptly it stopped again, firing down directly on Cara. She was shooting back with the Amban rifle, but Mando already knew she wouldn't last long.

"Take the bait, you hunk of junk," he muttered, and behind him, he heard Omera speaking to the others.

"It's now or never!" she said.

That was all the encouragement the other villagers needed. They sprang out of hiding and rushed forward to engage the bandits, as they'd been trained, in hand-to-hand combat—swinging staffs and spears, fighting back with everything they had. As the Mandalorian rose up to join them, he realized they might actually have a chance. If they could somehow manage to take out the walker. And that was an increasingly big *if*.

Cara stood up in the trench, the rifle at her shoulder, and fired a single shot into the right-side viewport of the AT-ST's command deck—a direct hit. The thing reared back as its red eye exploded in a shower of sparks, and the walker lurched forward, planting one foot over the edge of the trench, the dirt already beginning to crumble under its enormous weight.

That was all it took. Mando saw the walker's legs fold sideways and crumple underneath it, the upper control cabin hitting the ground with a deafening crash. He pulled out a gray charge, switched it on, and started running for the downed walker until he was close enough to toss the charge through the shattered viewport.

The explosion threw him headfirst into the trench. Rising up a moment later, he and Cara looked around to see what was left of the walker, and found its formerly imposing bulk reduced to a massive pile of flaming mechanical rubble.

The effect on the remaining bandits was almost immediate. With the AT-ST down, they suddenly found themselves on the losing end of the battle. The Mandalorian watched as they began turning around and running back into the woods, bellowing with dismay at how quickly they'd lost their advantage. Across the makeshift battlefield, he heard a cheer go up from the villagers as they raised their spears above their heads in victory.

You've earned it, he thought, and looked at Cara. "Was that the plan?"

She laughed, still trying to catch her breath. "Something like that."

CHAPTER

15

THE DAYS THAT FOLLOWED were some of the most restful Mando had experienced in recent memory. After the smoke cleared and the village returned to its normal rhythm, Mando found himself settling into his place in the barn. Omera continued to make them feel welcome, and the Child spent hours with Winta and the other children, playing and chasing swamp frogs.

The days blended together, and one afternoon, he and Cara Dune were outside the barn, watching as the Child caught a frog and popped it into his mouth so that its long legs wiggled and twitched from between his lips. The other children groaned in delight and disgust, and the Child spat out the frog and allowed it to hop away. A moment later, Omera came out to join them, watching the kids together.

"He's very happy here," she said.

Mando nodded. "He is."

"Fits right in." She smiled and walked away, going down to the krill pond. Cara glanced over at the bounty hunter.

"So, what happens if you take that thing off?" Cara asked. "They come after you and kill you?"

"No," he said. "You just can't ever put it back on again."

"That's it?" The former shock trooper looked at him in surprise. "So you can slip off the helmet and settle down with that beautiful young widow, and raise your kid sitting here, sipping spotchka?"

Mando didn't say anything for a moment. "You know," he said, "we raised some hell here, a few weeks back. It's too much action for a backwater town like this. Word travels fast." He looked over at her. "We might want to move on."

Cara gestured with her cup to where the children were gathered around the Child. "Wouldn't want to be the one who's gotta tell him," she said.

"I'm leaving him here," Mando said. "Traveling with me, that's no life for a kid. I did my job. He's safe. Better chance at a life."

"It's gonna break his little heart," Cara said, and took another drink from the cup in her hand.

"He'll get over it," Mando said. "We all do."

Before she could respond, he stood and left the porch, walking down toward the pond where Omera was kneeling down with a basket for the krill.

"Excuse me," he said. "Can I have a word?"

"Of course." She stood up to follow him away from the others. When Mando stopped, he realized he wasn't sure how to start the conversation.

"It's very nice here."

"Yes," Omera said.

"I think it's clear the kid's . . . he's happy here."

She smiled. "What about you?"

"Me?"

"Are you happy here?" When he didn't answer right away, she took in a breath. "We want you to stay. The community's grateful. You can pack all this away in case there's ever trouble." Her eyes searched for his behind the visor, gleaming softly in the afternoon light. "You and your boy could have a good life. He could be a child for a while." The gentleness of her voice seemed to blend with the general sense of peace that came out of the place, the people he'd come to know, the freedom they'd found there. "Wouldn't that be nice?"

"It would," Mando said.

Omera reached up with both hands and touched the sides of his helmet. He made no immediate move to remove her hands, not for several seconds. Finally, though, he took her wrists and guided them back down to her sides.

"I don't . . . belong here," he said, and glanced over at the Child. "But he does."

Omera swallowed and nodded. "I understand," she said. "I will look after him as one of my own."

"Thank you." He took a step back. "I should go."

He was turning to leave when a blaster shot rang out, sending flocks of startled birds up from the trees, jolting his thoughts, and setting the children screaming.

"Go get the kids!" Mando shouted at Omera, and drew his blaster, glancing down to make sure the Child was safe before running into the woods, in the direction of the shot.

He went scrambling between the trees, then up the slope. Reaching the place where the branches gave way to open air, he saw the outline of a figure standing at the top of the hill, blaster in hand.

It was Cara Dune.

The cloaked body at her feet was still smoking from the hole she'd put through it, a sniper rifle lying beside it. Mando reached down and flipped the body over, looking at the Kubaz bounty hunter's protective goggles and long snout. Mando saw the blinking tracker, still beeping its proximity alert. Cara was looking at him.

"Who's he tracking?" she asked.

"The kid."

She let out a breath. "They know he's here."

"Yes."

"Then they'll keep coming."

There was only one answer to that question. "Yes," the Mandalorian said. He brought his boot down hard on the

The Mandalorian is one of the greatest bounty hunters in the galaxy. He always gets his bounty.

The Mandalorian's ship is called the *Razor Crest*.

While searching for his bounty, Mando is helped by an Ugnaught named Kuiil.

Mando is surprised to discover that his bounty is just a child.

Mando returns the Child to the Client, but has a change of heart. He battles the Client's guards to get the Child back.

On the planet Sorgan, Mando encounters—and fights with—former rebel Cara Dune, but they are evenly matched.

The Child watches calmly as the Mandalorian and Cara Dune fight.

Mando and Cara Dune help Sorgan villagers fight off raiders who attack using an Imperial AT-ST walker.

On Tatooine, Mando teams up with a young bounty hunter named Toro Calican to track down the assassin Fennec Shand.

Fennec does her best to convince Toro to let her go.

The Child loves to eat frogs!

Mando realizes he needs to face the people who want the
Child, once and for all, and asks Cara Dune for help.

Greef Karga, Mando's contact in the Bounty Hunters Guild, pledges his help, as well, after the Child heals a wound on his arm.

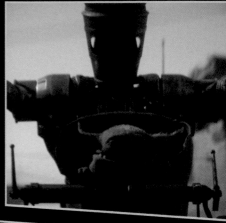

The Child is delighted as he and IG-11 zip along on a scout trooper's speeder.

Moff Gideon of the Empire arrives on Nevarro with stormtroopers, wanting the Child for himself.

The Armorer welds a signet onto the Mandalorian's armor.

IG-11 sacrifices himself so that Mando and the Child can make it to safety.

The Child knows that he can count on Mando to watch over him.

Although Mando and the Child escape . . . Moff Gideon, who wields the Darksaber, vows to find the Child.

The Mandalorian and the Child now form a clan of two!

tracking device, grinding it against the rocky ground until the red light went out.

Goodbyes took place by the supply sled that Mando was stocking up to take to the *Razor Crest*. Cara joined Omera, Winta, and the other villagers who had gathered as Mando finished loading supplies.

Cara stepped forward. "Until our paths cross," she said, offering a hand, and Mando took it.

"Until our paths cross." He glanced over at Winta, who was embracing the Child with tears in her eyes.

"I'm going to miss you so much," the girl said, and the Child hugged her back, chirping softly. When Mando looked up, he saw Omera in front of him.

"Thank you," she said. For a moment it seemed like she might say more, but in the end he just nodded, and he and the Child prepared to leave.

Moments later, they were gone.

CHAPTER

16

"**HAND OVER THE CHILD,** Mando, and I might let you live." The voice crackled through the *Razor Crest's* comm.

The Mandalorian realized the other ship was already on his tail, laser cannons firing close enough that the impact rocked the *Crest*. A second later, one of the shots hit the starboard engine, jolting the ship sideways and making the Child cry out with a startled whimper. Alarms blared, lights pulsing on the display in front of him, as the *Crest's* diagnostic systems reported serious damage.

"Hang on," Mando told the Child, bringing the weapons online and tilting into an evasive maneuver. The other ship was drawing closer, moving in for the kill. The pilot's voice was back in his ear, sounding cocky, overconfident.

"I can bring you in warm, or I can bring you in cold."

Mando let the would-be attacker close in, then hit the reverse thrusters and angled down, dropping abruptly back so the other ship swooped overhead, close enough to bounce off the *Crest's* left flank. Within less than a second, the Mandalorian had the other pilot locked in his sights.

"That's my line," he said, and squeezed the trigger.

Through the comm came a sudden startled scream. The ship exploded in front of him, pulverized into a million tiny scraps that were already vanishing into the surrounding blackness.

Settling back, he glanced at the Child, who was staring at him with wide-eyed amazement and—there was no denying it—enthusiastic delight.

"This isn't supposed to be fun," Mando said. The *Crest's* alarms were beeping, and he realized that the damage was worse than he'd initially thought. Some of the ship's systems were already failing, and it was losing fuel. They were going down fast.

He cut the engines, heard them sputter to a halt, and switched them on again, managing to coax the main thrusters back online . . . although it didn't sound promising.

Below, the reddish-brown sandscape of the planet in the distance was looming larger. Mando switched on his comm, hearing a voice already coming through:

"This is Mos Eisley tower," the voice said. "We are tracking you. Head for bay three-five, over."

"Copy that," Mando acknowledged. "Locked in for three-five."

By the time he landed, the left engine was spluttering again, fuming with ominous black smoke. Whatever was wrong with the thrusters already felt expensive. Extending the landing gear, he dropped the *Crest* down on the landing pad, sealed the Child in a secure compartment of the ship, and lowered the ramp to disembark.

The sign above the docking bay told him where he was:

TATOOINE

At the end of the boarding ramp, a series of electronic chirps and squeaks caught his attention. Three rusty-looking pit droids were bouncing eagerly toward him on their spindly legs, toolboxes in hand, like they were already preparing to dismantle the ship for scrap.

Mando drew his blaster and fired a warning shot, and the trio gave a communal squawk of terror before collapsing into flat protective shells.

"Hey!" someone shouted. Looking over, he saw a woman with curly brown hair in a one-piece coverall striding toward him, a tool belt swinging from around her waist. "You damage one of my droids, you'll pay for it."

"Just keep them away from my ship," Mando said.

"Yeah? You think that's a good idea, do you?" The woman eyed him speculatively. "Let's look at your ship." Approaching the *Crest*, she reached up and rapped one fist on the lower hull. The Mandalorian saw a piece of loose metal fall to the floor with a clatter. "Oof! Look at that," she said. "You've got a lot of carbon scoring up top. If I didn't know better, I'd think you were in a shootout."

Mando said nothing. She'd already brought out a hand-held diagnostic scope to take a better look at the damage. "Name's Peli Motto," she said, "since you didn't bother to ask. This is my operation. You're not gonna find a better mechanic on the planet." She leaned in farther, examining the underside of the engine. "Yeah, I'm gonna have to rotate that. You've got a fuel leak. Look at this, this is a mess. How did you even land?" Without waiting for an answer, she turned to Mando and got to the point: "That's gonna set you back."

"I've got five hundred Imperial credits," he said.

Motto looked unimpressed with the small bag of coins. "That's all you got? Well . . ." She looked back at the maintenance droids. "What do you guys think?"

The droids chirped, eyeing the bounty hunter cautiously and keeping their distance.

"Well, that should at least cover the hangar," Motto said.

"I'll get your money."

"Mm," she said. "I've heard that before."

"Just remember . . ." Mando said.

"Yeah," she said, "no droids. I heard ya. You don't have to say it twice."

He nodded and walked out of the hangar.

———

The streets of Mos Eisley were mostly empty, as if whatever had happened on the planet had been over long before. Low, single-story dwellings the color of sandstone faced one another in relative silence.

Going around a corner and down the next street, Mando glanced up and saw a group of Imperial stormtrooper helmets suspended on spikes jutting out of the ground, a grim monument and a reminder that the Empire no longer held the planet in its grip . . . and perhaps a warning to anyone who might think otherwise. Farther along he encountered some of the rubble from the last skirmish that had taken place there, damaged equipment that looked like it had taken heavy fire. There were a few more inhabitants there, and a nearby doorway led to a cantina.

He stepped into the darkness.

Inside was a largely empty establishment with a pair of service droids making drinks behind the bar and a series of tables along the wall where a handful of others—drifters and pilots of all different species—were conferring in murmurs. There was an empty bandstand with no sign of musicians. Like the street outside, it looked like the sort of place that had seen action in the past, in another lifetime; it was easy to imagine rollicking music being played there, the place alive with activity and intrigue, promises and threats. No longer.

"Hey, droid," he said, approaching the bar. "I'm a hunter. I'm looking for work."

The droid did not look up from the glass it was wiping out. "Unfortunately, the Bounty Guild no longer operates from Tatooine."

"I'm not looking for Guild work."

"I am afraid that does not improve your situation," it said, "at least by my calculation."

"Think again, tin can," said a man at one of the tables behind Mando.

He turned to look at the young man sitting in the shadows, his feet propped up in front of him in a gesture of supreme self-confidence.

"If you're looking for work, have a seat, my friend." He didn't wait for the Mandalorian to respond. "Name's Toro, Toro Calican." He gestured to the empty seat across from him. "Come on, relax."

The Mandalorian had barely sat down across from him when Calican slapped a puck on the table with a flourish, activating the holo in front of him.

"Picked up this bounty puck before I left the Mid Rim," the kid said, clearly pleased with himself. "Fennec Shand, an assassin. Heard she's been on the run ever since the New Republic put all her employers in lockdown."

Mando gazed down at the face of the woman, her features cool and remote, sniper's eyes that were dark and devoid of mercy, even in the holo. "I know the name," he said.

"Yeah, well, I followed this tracking fob here," Calican

said casually, holding it up to display the blinking red light. "Now the data suggests she's headed out beyond the Dune Sea. Should be an easy job."

Mando rose to his feet. "Well, good luck with that."

For a second Calican was too surprised to speak. "Wait, wait, wait, hey, I thought you needed work?"

"How long have you been with the Guild?"

"Long enough."

"Clearly not." Mando nodded at the puck. "Fennec Shand is an elite mercenary. She made her name killing for all the top crime syndicates. Including the Hutts." He met the younger man's gaze. "If you go after her, you won't make it past sunrise."

He began to walk away, already thinking of what his next stop would be. Mos Eisley might've been a sleepy town without much to recommend it, but there was always an opportunity for those who were motivated enough to look. And he needed to pay for those repairs, to get moving again as soon as possible.

"Wait," Calican blurted out.

Mando turned back and saw that the young hunter was looking at him differently, all the cockiness and poise slipping away to reveal the lack of experience beneath.

"This is my first job," Calican admitted. "You can keep the money, all of it. I just . . . need this job to get into the Guild." He shook his head. "I can't do it alone."

The Mandalorian said nothing for a long moment. "Meet me at hangar three-five in half an hour," he said finally, and saw the kid already relaxing again. "Bring two speeder bikes, and give me the tracking fob."

Calican held the fob out, as if he were going to put it in Mando's hand, and then smashed it against the wall instead. The grin was back on his face as if it had never left.

"Don't worry," he said. "I've got it all memorized." The grin widened. "Looks like you're stuck with me now, partner!"

"Half an hour." Before the kid could say anything more, Mando turned and walked away.

CHAPTER

17

AFTER LEAVING the cantina, Mando walked back to the hangar bay, to the *Razor Crest*, and went aboard the vessel, making his way back to the compartment where he'd hidden the Child.

But the Child wasn't there.

Mando turned and ran down the ship's ramp. "Hey!"

Inside her office, Peli Motto jerked upright and raised her head, shouting, "I'm awake! I'm awake!"

"Where is he?"

"Quiet!" She came out, holding the Child and bouncing him in her arms, and glared at him. "You woke it up! Do you have any idea how long it took me to get it to sleep?"

"Give him to me."

Instead, Motto stood her ground and glared at him, with the Child clutched protectively in her arms. "Not so fast! You can't just leave a child all alone like that." She scowled with disapproval and maternal instinct. "You know, you have an awful lot to learn about raising a young one."

The Mandalorian looked down at the Child, who had stopped crying and was gazing up at Motto, babbling contentedly in her arms.

"Anyway," Motto went on, "I started the repair on the fuel leak. I had a couple setbacks I want to talk to you about." Shifting the Child easily into the crook of her left elbow, she reached up to the wall console, flipped open the access panel, and typed in a diagnostic code. The Child observed all this with vivid interest. "You know I didn't use any droids, as requested, so it took me a lot longer than I expected." She glanced hesitantly at him. "But I figured you were good for the money, since you have an extra mouth to feed."

Mando glanced back to the Child again, hearing him coo and gurgle. The kid seemed to recognize that, whatever Peli Motto's financial motives might be, he was safe with her.

"Thank you," he said.

The earnestness of his response seemed to surprise her, but only briefly. "Oh, well, I guess I was right," she said. "You got a job, didn't you?" He didn't need to reply, but she followed him outside, still talking. "You know, it's costing me a lot of money to keep these droids even powered up!"

The Mandalorian stopped. In front of him, Toro Calican stood next to a pair of speeder bikes that floated effortlessly above their own shadows. The young hunter was leaning against one of the bikes with his arms crossed, head tilted back in a pose that he'd no doubt practiced in a hundred different mirrors.

He gestured at the bikes. "Hey, Mando, what do you think?"

He inspected the bikes cautiously, not expecting much. They were secondhand at best, mashed together out of spare parts, but they'd make it to the Dune Sea.

"What do you expect?" Calican asked defensively. "This isn't Corellia," he said, referring to the planet known for top-of-the-line ship manufacturing. He turned to nod at Motto, who was still standing there with the Child in her arms. "Ma'am."

Peli Motto said nothing, just gave him the suspicious glance of one who'd seen his kind come and go, but Mando heard the Child's response, a bright chuckle of amusement, as if all this—including Toro Calican's posturing—was just part of a pageant that had been arranged for his personal entertainment.

Mando climbed aboard his bike. Calican had already fired up his engine and gone roaring down the street toward the desert, and a moment later, the Mandalorian joined him, hoping that he wasn't making a mistake.

He'd find out soon enough.

CHAPTER

18

THE DESERT WAS FOREVER.

For the archaeologists who studied its past, the Dune Sea contained countless secrets. Folklore held that, once, long before, it had been an actual sea, before the twin suns of Tatooine had dried it up and left it as it stood, hundreds of kilometers of blazing hot sand that stretched out in all directions. Bones of creatures long since extinct littered the dunes, and beneath them, perhaps, lay ancient kingdoms that had come and gone even before that.

The Mandalorian pushed the throttle forward, leaning into the wind. The speeder bike performed better than he'd expected, its engines actually seeming to function best at top speed, as if appreciating an opportunity to devour so much open space.

Somewhere out there was their target: Fennec Shand.

Shand's reputation was beyond question. For those who could afford her services—crime lords, crooked politicians, and Hutts—she was a messenger of death, a ghost with a sniper rifle, and by the time you saw her, it was already too late.

Mando knew that if they failed in their mission to bring her back, he and Calican would never survive. Shand would make sure of that.

Throttling down the speeder bike, he slowed and came to a halt. The kid stopped alongside him and peeled off his goggles, glancing over. "What's going on?"

Mando pointed. "Look. Up ahead."

Calican climbed off his bike and pulled a pair of macrobinoculars from his pack, aiming them at a pair of banthas that were standing unattended in the distance. "Tusken Raiders," he sneered. "I heard the locals talking about this filth."

"Tuskens think they're the locals," Mando said. "Everyone else is just trespassing."

The kid snorted as if he would've expected as much from an inferior species. "Well, whatever they call themselves, they best keep their distance."

"Yeah? Why don't you tell them yourself."

Calican turned around, ready with some offhand retort, and saw the two Tuskens standing behind him, their traditional gaffi sticks in hand. His mouth fell open and his eyes went wide.

"Relax," Mando said. He turned to the Tuskens, raising his hands and addressing them in sign language.

"What are you doing?"

The Mandalorian didn't bother looking over at him. "Negotiating."

"For what?" The kid looked back and forth, bewildered, as the Tusken in front of them responded, the conversation drawing out in silence. "What's going on?"

"We're going to need passage across their land," Mando said. A moment later, he turned to Calican. "Let me see the binocs."

"Why?"

Without bothering to respond, Mando took the macro-binoculars, turned, and tossed them to the Tusken, who caught them easily and tucked them away.

"Hey!" Calican bawled. "Those were brand new!"

"Yeah, they were." Mando got back on his bike, revved the engine, and took off, not waiting for the kid to follow.

They rode farther, coming up alongside a high dune, and Mando cut the speeder's power and leapt off, gesturing for Calican to follow. "Get down."

"What? Oh." The kid dismounted, scrambling to join him.

Crouched down side by side, they peered into the open

valley below. The arid silence was pierced by the faint but unmistakable bray of an animal wandering in the middle distance.

"All right," Mando said, "tell me what you see."

"Dewback," Calican said, gazing down at the bellowing lizard, which was dragging a body behind it in its harness, facedown in the sand. "Looks like the rider's still attached." He glanced at the Mandalorian. "Is that her? Is that the target?"

"I don't know." Mando drew his blaster. "I'll go. You cover me. Stay down."

The kid didn't argue, just nodded and pulled his own weapon. Mando rose up and went running down the dune, heading for the dewback and into plain sight.

As he got closer, the lizard seemed to grow more skittish, trying to get away from him. Something had the dewback spooked, and it jerked harder at the body that was tethered to it, braying and whinnying restlessly. Mando raised one hand. "Whoa, whoa," he said, and approached the body, kneeling down to turn it over and look at it. The dead man's face was unfamiliar, but he was well outfitted with navigation and survival tech, weapons and tracking gear—tools of the trade the Mandalorian recognized immediately.

"Is it her?" Calican called out from behind the dune. "Is she dead?"

Mando was still looking at the equipment. "It's another bounty hunter."

"Hey, I hope you don't plan on keeping all that stuff for yourself," Calican shouted. "Can I at least have that blaster?"

Mando found the tracking fob. It was hanging from the dead man's belt, blinking and beeping rapidly. All his senses sharpened, and the world suddenly seemed to go very still. He straightened up and swung around to look at the kid.

"Get down!" he shouted, and the sniper bolt came slashing out of the distance and smashed into him, knocking him off his feet.

He jumped up and started full-out sprinting for the dune, head down and feet pounding across the loose sand, already feeling the target on his back. If it was Shand who'd fired the first round, then the moment between shots wasn't hesitation—she was simply taking her time to get him perfectly in her sights.

Wham! The next shot hit him squarely in the back, throwing him over the edge and sending him rolling down the other side.

"Mando!" the kid shouted. He sounded scared but excited, too, ready to move but unsure what was happening.

Mando caught his breath and crawled back up to join him. The armor had taken the brunt of the hit and saved his life, but the impact of the bolt still had to go somewhere. He felt like he was back on Arvala-7 getting tossed around by the mudhorn.

"What happened?" Calican asked.

"Sniper bolt." The Mandalorian peered back down to where he'd been standing a moment earlier. "Only an MK-modified rifle could make that shot."

The kid stared at him. "Are you all right?"

"Yeah. Hit me in the beskar," he said, "and at that range, beskar held up."

"Wait." Calican blinked. "I don't wear any beskar."

"Nope."

"So, what do we do?"

"You see where that shot came from?"

"Yeah." The kid pointed. "It came from that ridge."

"Okay." The plan was formulating in his mind. "We're gonna wait until dark."

"Well, what if she escapes?"

"She's got the high ground. She'll wait for us to make the first move." Rising up, Mando began to make his way down the sheltered side of the dune where they'd parked the speeder bikes. "I'm gonna rest. You take the first watch." He thought back on the enthusiasm in the kid's voice once the shooting had started, that rookie's instinct to react first and think later. "Stay low!"

Time passed slowly, shadows creeping across ripples of sand as Tatooine's twin suns edged over the horizon, receding into mingled shades of orange, red, and purple, and finally vanished completely. The darkness that followed was cool at first, then almost startlingly cold.

In the darkness, the Mandalorian opened his eyes and emerged from what hadn't really been sleep. Calican, however, clearly thought he was dozing. The kid was coming down the dune, speaking in a voice loud enough that the older bounty hunter would've thought he wanted Shand to hear him.

"All right, suns are down. Time to ride, Mando."

Mando didn't move, letting the kid come closer.

"Look at you," Calican scoffed, his voice tinged with scorn. "Asleep on the job, old man." Chuckling, he stepped back, then whipped around, drawing his blaster and pointing with a grin before spinning it on his finger and posing.

Mando turned to him. "You done?"

"Huh?" The grin vanished, and the blaster went back in its holster. "Yeah, yeah, I was just, you know, waking you up. Come on."

The Mandalorian rose to his feet. "Get on your bike," he said, and pointed. "Ride as fast as you can toward those rocks."

"That's your plan?" Calican snorted. "She'll snipe us right off the bikes."

Mando reached into his pack and plucked out a small rectangular device. He tossed it to the kid. "It's a flash charge," he said. "We alternate shots. It'll blind any scope temporarily. Combine that with our speed and we got a chance."

"A *chance*?"

"Hey, you wanted this," Mando reminded him. "Get ready."

They revved the speeder engines and went over the dune.

At first, the plan went perfectly. Riding hard for the rocks, Mando raised one arm and set off his flash charge, sending a blinding pulse of energy streaking upward into the blackness, casting weird, angled shadows along the ground beneath them. In its glow, he could see the kid beside him out of the corner of his eye and gave him the nod. "Go!"

Calican set off his flash charge. Again the night sky shuddered and pulsed with piercing white light. They kept going, roaring forward, still gaining speed. The rocks were closer, and Mando thought he could make out a shape with a sniper rifle and helmet in the middle distance, trying to get a clean shot.

But Calican's next flash charge never made it into the sky. Somehow it went wild, corkscrewing sideways before fizzling out along the dunes. Too late, Mando realized what it meant. The misfire had given Shand the opening she needed—just enough darkness to draw a bead on them and triangulate the shot.

Blam!

He heard the sniper bolt at the same time he felt it, hammering him off his bike and into the sand. The bike shot forward unattended for a moment before wiping out somewhere in the blackness.

Sprawled in the dirt, he had the presence of mind to raise one hand and fire off another flash charge, just before Shand could take the kill shot. Or so he thought.

The blast hit him squarely in the chest, and for an instant, everything dissolved into a cool black void. A second later, he sat up, his head spinning, hearing grunts and groans, punches and kicks not far from him. From the sound of it, Calican was getting his brains beaten in.

Mando drew his blaster and walked over, pointing it down at Shand. "Nice distraction," he told Calican.

When Fennec Shand realized what had happened, she stopped fighting and raised her hands. Calican stood up and caught his breath. "Yeah," the kid said, and nodded at Mando. "Good work, partner."

The Mandalorian didn't take his eyes off of Shand. He tossed a pair of binders to where she was still kneeling. "Cuff yourself," he said, and when she did, he glanced at Calican. "Why don't you go find your blaster?"

The kid walked off without a word. As he left, Shand looked up at Mando, regarding him with interest.

"A Mandalorian," she said, pronouncing the word as if it

were an exotic species. "It's been a long time since I've seen one of your kind." A slight smile rose to her face. "Ever been to Nevarro?"

He said nothing.

"I heard things didn't go so well there," Shand said casually, "but it looks like you got off easy. Not so much as a scratch on the pretty new beskar. Well"—she pointed with her chin at the blaster marks that the sniper bolts had left on his armor—"maybe a dent or two."

"You won't have to worry about getting to Nevarro or anywhere else, once we turn you in," Calican said as he walked over, brushing the sand from his blaster and returning the weapon to its holster. He looked down at her in the darkness. "You know, I really should thank you. You're my ticket into the Guild."

"You're welcome," Shand said dryly.

The three of them walked over to the one remaining speeder bike, and Mando heard her chuckle.

"Uh-oh. Looks like one of us has to walk."

"Or we could drag you," Mando said. He gave the kid a *follow me* look, and led him out of Shand's earshot, the two of them speaking in lowered voices.

"Okay," Calican said, "so what *is* the plan?"

"I need you to go find that dewback we saw," Mando told him.

The kid's eyebrows shot up in disbelief. "And leave you here, with my bounty and my ride?" He shook his head. "Yeah, I don't think so, Mando."

The Mandalorian turned to look out on the desert, weighing his options.

"Okay," he said. "I'll do it." He looked back over at Shand. "Watch her, and don't let her get near the bike. She's no good to us dead."

After the Mandalorian left, Toro Calican sat on the remaining bike, waiting, while Shand stayed in her place on the ground. The night seemed to go on forever. At first he'd thought she might try to escape, but after a while he realized this was just as boring as he'd feared it would be. All the glamour of the job was over. The rest was just waiting.

Waiting, and getting paid.

Finally, as dawn broke over the desert, Shand sighed and stretched. "Oh, look, the suns are coming up."

Calican didn't look up from his boots. "Quiet."

"Look, there's still time to make my rendezvous in Mos Espa," she said. "Take me to it, and I can pay you double the price on my head."

He snorted. "I don't care about the money."

"So the Mandalorian gets all the credits?" she asked. "Is that your idea of a fair deal?"

"I hired Mando. This is my job." Calican looked at her. "Bringing you in will make me a full member of the Bounty Hunters Guild."

Shand raised her eyebrows. "You already have something the Guild values far more than me," she said. "You just don't see it."

"What?"

"The Mandalorian. His armor alone's worth more than my bounty. And think what it would do for your reputation." She waited, letting him put the pieces together for himself. "A Mandalorian shot up the Guild on Nevarro. Took some high-value target and went rogue."

Calican wasn't bothering to hide his interest anymore, pointing out into the desert with his blaster. "*That* Mandalorian?"

"You don't see many," Shand said. "You bring the Guild that traitor, and they'll welcome you with open arms. Your name will be legendary."

Calican got off the bike and walked over to her. "How can we be sure he's the one?"

"Word is, he's still got the target with him," Shand said. "Some say it's a child." She leaned forward. "Look, if you're afraid to take him on, fear not. I can help you with that." She could tell that he was listening attentively, very close to making a decision. "You want to be a bounty hunter? Take some advice. Make the best deal for yourself, and survive."

Calican drew in a deep breath, holstered his blaster, and walked closer. Shand stood up to meet him, extending her arms so he could remove the binders.

He paused, looking at her, then drew the blaster again and fired, hitting her squarely in the chest. Shand made an almost inaudible choking sound. At first the shock was greater than the pain. But then the pain came.

"That's good advice," Calican was saying, from what seemed like very far away, "but if I took those binders off you, I'd be a dead man." He nodded. "And if the Mandalorian's worth more than you are, then who wouldn't want to be a legend?" A slight smile touched the corner of his mouth. "Thanks for the tip."

The last thing Fennec Shand saw before consciousness slipped away was the kid turning and walking to the bike, then riding toward the horizon.

Tracking the dewback in the dark took longer than Mando had expected. He could only imagine how long it would've taken the kid. By the time he finally caught up with the great lizard and rode it back to the ridgeline, the bike was gone.

Mando sat astride the dewback for a moment, looking down at Fennec Shand's body, still cuffed, lying motionless on the ground.

Mando sighed. Then he turned the dewback around and started the long ride back.

CHAPTER

19

RIDING INTO MOS EISLEY, the Mandalorian approached the hangar and saw the kid's bike parked out front. He stopped and looked at it.

He drew his blaster and eased through the entry point, into the silence of the hangar bay. The *Razor Crest* was there, its ramp lowered, but there was no sign of Peli Motto, the pit droids, or anyone else. Mando eased around the corner, listening for the scuff of a footstep or the sound of a breath.

Nothing. Off to the left, he heard a frantic squawk, and he saw one of Motto's droids scamper across the floor toward the sanctuary of her office, where the other two droids were already cowering. Mando walked toward the center of the bay, the blaster still held out in front of him.

"Took you long enough, Mando." The kid's voice rang out from inside the *Crest*'s opening hatch. When the Mandalorian looked, the first thing he saw was Peli Motto coming down out of the shadows. Her expression was pinched and frightened, and behind her he saw the Child's face, the fearful gleam of those big eyes seeming to float in the darkness. Finally Calican emerged, and Mando saw that he was carrying the Child in one hand and pointing a blaster at Motto's back with the other. Calican walked the rest of the way down until the three were in front of Mando.

"Looks like I'm calling the shots now, huh, partner?" he asked. "Drop your blaster and raise 'em."

Mando tossed the blaster to the floor, then raised his hands, putting them behind his head. He heard the Child make a soft, worried cry.

"Cuff him," Calican said to Motto.

She gave a disgusted grunt and walked forward to put the binders on him while the young bounty hunter leveled his blaster at the Mandalorian's head.

"You're a Guild traitor, Mando," Calican said, and gestured to the Child in his arms. "And I'm willing to bet that this here is the target you helped escape."

The Mandalorian didn't respond. The kid had been rehearsing this speech, his big moment of triumph, and he was so caught up in what he was saying that he didn't notice the flash charge in Mando's hand. But Peli Motto saw it as she went around behind him with the binders, and he heard her whisper: "You're smarter than you look."

"Fennec was right," Calican continued. "Bringing you in won't just make me a member of the Guild"—his voice softened—"it'll make me *legendary*."

He aimed the blaster directly at Mando's face.

Mando triggered the flash.

The entire hangar erupted in a blinding pulse of light. Calican cried out in surprise, wincing, and retreated back up the ramp of the *Crest*, aiming frantically around the hangar while he waited for his eyes to adjust. But when his vision finally cleared, the Mandalorian wasn't there. He fired almost randomly, hitting nothing.

Mando stepped forward, raised his blaster, and pulled the trigger. It only took one shot. Toro Calican collapsed and fell off the ramp, landing face-first on the hangar floor.

Mando kept his blaster up. "Stay back," he said as he approached the body, but Peli Motto wasn't listening.

"We've gotta get it," she said as the Mandalorian rolled Calican's body over. For a moment they both stood, confused. The Child was gone.

"Where is it?" Motto asked.

Behind them, Mando heard a soft gurgling sound. He looked around and saw one long ear protruding from behind some equipment as the Child peered up at them from his hiding place.

"There you are," Motto said as she knelt down in front

of him. The Child responded with a happy series of chirps and an upraised hand. "Are you hiding from us? Huh?" She scooped him up. "That's all right. I know, that was really loud for your big old ears, wasn't it?"

As she cradled the Child and reassured him that everything was going to be fine, Mando bent down over Calican's body. The kid was a victim of his own mistakes, all of them leading up to one last, fatal error in judgment. Calican had been greedy, but it was recklessness that got him killed.

He lifted the sack of coins from the kid's pocket, weighed it in his hand, and walked over to where Motto was holding the Child.

"Be careful with him," she said, passing the gurgling infant into the bounty hunter's arms. Then her voice toughened into the more familiar sound of a backwater mechanic. "So, I take it you didn't get paid?"

Mando brought out the sack and turned it upside down, filling Motto's palms until they were overflowing with credits. "Will that cover me?"

The astonished look on her face was answer enough until she managed to form words. "Yeah. Yeah, this is gonna cover you."

As he carried the Child up the ramp and aboard the *Razor Crest*, Mando heard Motto, still standing over Calican's body, yell, "All right, pit droids, let's drag this out of here!"

One of the droids squawked out a question. "I don't know, drag it to Beggar's Canyon!"

Inside the cockpit, he switched on the engines and heard them both firing up with a familiar, encouraging roar. Motto had done good work—if it had been Motto, and not her droids, who'd finished the repairs. Either way, the results spoke for themselves, and they were underway in no time.

CHAPTER

20

"MANDO," THE BEARDED MAN said. "Is that you under that bucket?"

The Mandalorian looked at the well-worn, grinning face surrounded by bushy hair, the gleaming eyes, the outstretched hand. "Ran," he said, and took the man's hand, shaking it.

"I didn't know if I'd ever see you in these parts again," Ranzar Malk said, still smiling. They were standing in the docking bay of the Roost, the space station where Mando had arrived looking for work. "Good to see you. To be honest, I was a little surprised when you reached out to me. Because I . . . I hear things." Ran raised an eyebrow and lowered his voice, inviting confidence. "Like maybe things between you and the Guild ain't working out?"

"I'll be fine," Mando said evenly.

Ran shrugged. "Okay," he said. "You know the policy. No questions. And you"—the smile returned, and he rested a companionable hand on Mando's shoulder—"you're welcome back here anytime." He gestured to an elevated walkway. "Come on. Let's take a walk."

The Mandalorian followed him along the walkway, the two of them making their way above the various fighters and freighters that had settled in for maintenance. Sparks flew from soldering irons and power tools, raising odorous clouds of smoke. This was a busy place, and there was no shortage of ships awaiting repair.

"So what's the job?" Mando asked.

"Well," Ran said, "one of our associates ran afoul of some competitors and got himself caught. I'm putting together a crew to spring him. It's a five-person job. I got four." He turned to look at Mando. "All I need is the ride, and you brought it."

They stopped walking. The bounty hunter gazed down at his ship on the pad below. "The ship wasn't part of the deal," he said.

"Well, the *Crest* is the only reason I let you back in here." Ran's seemingly cheerful expression hadn't changed. "What's the look? Is that gratitude?" He laughed. "Uh-huh, I think it is."

He was still chuckling as he turned and walked away.

Down below, the Mandalorian met the rest of Ran's crew, starting with a bald, smirking man named Mayfeld, who wore a specially made blaster prosthetic in a shoulder rig, where he could make sure everybody saw it.

Mayfeld looked Mando up and down, unimpressed, before turning to Ran. "This is the guy you were telling me about?"

"Mando and I used to do jobs together back in the day," Ran said. "We were all young, trying to make a name for ourselves, but running with a Mandalorian, that was"—he glanced over at Mando—"that brought us some reputation." He gave a gruff, nostalgic chortle. "We did some crazy stuff, didn't we?"

"That was a long time ago," Mando said.

"Well, I don't go out anymore," Ran said, "so Mayfeld, he's gonna run point on this job." His voice grew more serious. "If he says it, it's like it's coming from me. You good with that?"

"You tell me," Mando said, and saw Mayfeld's reaction, the man's eyebrows rising.

Ran burst out laughing again. "You haven't changed one bit."

"Well, things have changed around here," Mayfeld blustered, and turned to swagger away, making sure that Mando saw he was taking his time about it.

"Mayfeld's one of the best triggermen I've ever seen," Ran said. "Former Imperial sharpshooter."

"That's not saying much," Mando said.

Mayfeld looked over his shoulder. "I wasn't a storm-trooper!"

Ran glanced at his old friend with another rueful laugh. "Doesn't take much, does it?" he said. "Come on, you might as well meet the rest of them."

Down by the *Razor Crest*, Mando found himself surrounded by the other members of the team—the massive, standoffish Devaronian named Burg; the bug-eyed droid named Zero; and bringing up the rear, a purple-skinned female Twi'lek whose voice the Mandalorian recognized even before he saw her face.

"Hello, Mando," she said.

"Xi'an," he said.

"Tell me why I shouldn't cut you down where you stand?" she asked, and lunged at him, dagger in hand, thrusting it up underneath his helmet.

He didn't flinch. "Nice to see you, too," he said, and the laughter of the others faded as Xi'an leaned in closer, turning her head and clicking her tongue.

"I've *missed* you," she whispered, gazing into his visor as if she could somehow see more than just her own eyes staring back at her—or maybe that's all she wanted to see.

Mayfeld brought the team together and ran down the plan. "The package is being moved on a fortified transport ship," he said, indicating the pale blue holodisplay that he'd activated in front of him. "We've got a limited window to board, find our friend, get him out of there before they make their jump."

Mando looked at the three-dimensional diagram hovering below him and recognized the design. "That's a New Republic prison ship," he said, and looked at Mayfeld. "Your man wasn't taken by a rival syndicate. He was *arrested*."

"So what?" Mayfeld asked.

Ran looked at Mando. "A job is a job," he reminded him.

"That's a max-security transport," Mando said. "I'm not looking for that kind of heat."

"Why do you think we're using the *Razor Crest*?" Ran said. "It's not much to look at, but it's off the old Imperial and New Republic grid. It's a ghost. They'll never see it coming."

They waited while Mayfeld explained the rest. "We'll drop out of hyperspace close enough to get in their blind spot," he said. "We'll have just enough time to scramble their signal."

"That's not possible," Mando said. "Even for the *Crest*."

Ran grinned and gestured to the droid. "That's why he's flying." Anticipating the Mandalorian's response, he held up one hand. "I know you're a good pilot, but this time we need you on the trigger, not on the wheel. Zero may be a little rough around the edges, but he's the best."

Mando waited as Zero followed the rest of the team aboard the ship, until it was just him and Ran standing at the foot of the ramp. "How can you trust it?" he asked.

"You know me, Mando," Ran said. "I don't trust anybody."

Mando started up the gangplank to his ship and heard Ran speak up behind him.

"Just like the good old days, huh, Mando?"

The Mandalorian looked around and said nothing. Reaching out, he hit the switch to withdraw the ramp and close the hatch, then watched Ran's bearded face, still grinning, until it was gone. He could hear the engines throttling up and realized that meant the droid was already in the cockpit, starting preflight programming.

For better or worse, it was time to go.

CHAPTER

21

THE TROUBLE BEGAN when the Devaronian tried to take Mando's helmet off.

They had just made the jump to hyperspace, and Zero was flying, which meant nobody had anything better to do than wait around belowdecks. Mando had caught them rummaging through his arsenal, and Mayfeld told Burg it might be time to see what the Mandalorian looked like under his bucket. When the Devaronian made a move to grab it and lift it off, Mando smashed him hard in the face, knowing he'd have to land as many punches as he could early to get any kind of advantage. Otherwise it wouldn't even be a fight— Burg would simply pick him up and snap him in half.

That didn't happen, but only because the Devaronian fell back and hit the control switch on the wall, opening the hatchway behind him. There was a quick whoosh, and the bounty hunter heard the Child inside chirp in surprise.

Everyone stopped.

"Whoa." Mayfeld stared at the Child, rising to his feet. "What is *that*?" He glanced at Mando, eyes bright, then back at the Child. "What is it, like a pet or something?"

"Yeah," the Mandalorian said carefully. "Something like that."

Mayfeld nodded, as if they'd finally found some common ground. "Me, I was never into pets. I mean, I tried, but it didn't work out. But I'm thinking"—he reached down and lifted the Child up—"maybe I'll try again with this little fella." He was looking at Mando, the Child held out in front of him, and opened his hands, pretending to drop him.

Mando didn't move. Mayfeld waited to see what would happen, thinking that if the bounty hunter tried anything, there would be one extra share he and the others could divide among them, and they could all fly home in the ship. Ran would be happy to have it.

"Coming out of hyperspace now." Zero's voice through the intercom interrupted, and it was time to go to work.

"Commence extraction now," the droid said.

It had been a rough landing, turbulent enough to throw them all sideways and backward as Zero completed the coupling with the transport. The Mandalorian rose to his feet and heard Mayfeld's voice behind him. "All right, we've got a job to do," he said. "Mando, you're up."

The Mandalorian bent down over the *Crest*'s ventral

hatchway, rigging the bypass cable to the other ship's dock-ing port, which was locked from the inside. The red light on the console spluttered and flickered as the system scanned the prison ship's security code and triggered it. The light on the console turned green, and the hatch opened with a vacuum-sealed whoosh.

Just like that, they were in.

Inside, the prison ship was a desolate maze of long white corridors lined with cells, the hallways stretching out in dif-ferent directions, empty except for a pair of patrol droids. Mayfeld keyed the comm. "Zero, get us to the control room."

"Sublevel three," the droid replied promptly from the *Crest*. "Disabling onboard surveillance."

"All right," Mayfeld said, "we're on the clock. The second we engage those droids, they're gonna be all over us."

"I know the drill," the Mandalorian said.

Blaster raised, the bald man led the way down the hall, and the others followed in silence. They walked past cells where inmates dangled their hands through the bars, gazing at them and making curious noises.

"I don't like this," Mando said.

"You always were paranoid," Xi'an jeered.

Mayfeld raised an eyebrow. "Is that true, Mando? Were you always *paranoid*?"

To their left, something inside one of the cells roared and slammed against the door hard enough to make them draw away from it—except for Xi'an, who leaned in and hissed back at it, making Burg chortle. Zero's voice came through the communicator again.

"Approaching control room," the droid said. "Make a left at the next juncture."

As they went around the corner, a small mouse droid swerved across the floor in front of them. "It's just a little mousey," the Devaronian said, drawing his blaster and hiding it behind his back. "Come here, little mousey. . . ."

The droid hesitated and started to back away, and Burg snarled. Whipping out his blaster, he fired, blowing it apart.

"What are you doing?" Mayfeld said. "You're gonna—"

It was already too late. The hallway in front of them filled with four security droids, marching forward, their blasters blazing. Mando and the others took cover along the walls and tried to return fire, but it was almost impossible without exposing themselves. Mayfeld's shoulder piece extended a blaster on its mechanical arm, firing from behind him, but the security droids just kept attacking.

"Mando, let's go! You're supposed to be something special." Mayfeld shook his head in disappointment. "I *knew* it!"

Then the Mandalorian ran forward, going into a low slide at the last second, hitting the droids low, and knocking one of them over. He sprang up, grabbed the nearest one, and smashed its head against the floor, then fired his cable at another and pulled, yanking the droid forward and flinging it into the opposite wall. The others tried to react, but their mechanical bodies were too big and awkward for that kind of close-quarters fighting. They were still struggling to catch up as the Mandalorian ripped a chunk of the chest plate from one, whipped around, and threw it into the head of the other, impaling it. The fight ended when he used a razor coil to decapitate the last droid standing, sending its metal head rattling to the floor—

And then two more burst in, guns at the ready. The bounty hunter unleashed his blowtorches on them, incinerating the body of one and firing a blaster through the other.

In the silence, Mando could hear the prisoners whooping and cheering in their cells. It wasn't every day they were treated to the sound of a half dozen security droids being reduced to parts. Mayfeld was less impressed. He led the others past the Mandalorian as they stepped over the scattered pieces of mech.

"Make sure you clean up your mess," Mayfeld muttered.

But when they reached the control room, the mess just got worse.

"There were only supposed to be droids on this ship," Mando said as they stood in front of an anxious, and very human, corrections officer, who was pointing his blaster back at them. In his other hand, the officer held a tracking beacon, and they all knew what that meant. Once activated, a New

Republic attack team would home in on the signal and end the job abruptly, along with their lives.

It was Mando who spoke first. "Put it down," he told the guard, whose frightened face showed only faint signs that he was actually listening. "We're not here for you. We're here for the prisoner."

The guard didn't budge. Mayfeld wouldn't lower his blaster, either. It was Xi'an who ended the standoff by knocking the officer out and dropping him to the floor.

"Would you both just shut up?" she said.

Mayfeld looked down at the tracker, lying on the floor where the guard had dropped it. Its light was blinking.

"Was that thing blinking before?" he asked, voice trembling. "*Was* it?"

Zero came through the communicator, answering the question for him. "I've detected a New Republic tracking signal," the droid said, "homing in on your location. You have approximately twenty minutes."

Xi'an cocked her head and licked her lips, her eyes shimmering with excitement. "We only need five."

When they reached the cell, Zero activated remote access, and the door lifted to reveal a Twi'lek male seated on the bench inside.

"Brother," Xi'an said, smiling.

"Sister," the male Twi'lek said, grinning back. He stared

out at the Mandalorian with cold, familiar eyes. "And look who else came along for the ride."

"Qin," Mando said in greeting.

"Funny," the Twi'lek said, stepping outside to join the others in the hallway without ever breaking eye contact with Mando. "The man who left me behind is now my savior."

Behind him, Mando heard a growl. As he turned, Burg punched him hard enough to hurl him into the vacant cell. Mando spun around and fired back at them, but the door was already closing. The blaster bolt ricocheted around the walls, skimming past his head. He heard the cell's locking device click into place.

He was sealed inside.

After the others left, a security droid moved past the cell. Mando reached out, fired his grappling cable, and snared the droid around the neck, then yanked it up against the other side of the door. He grabbed the droid's arm and twisted, feeling the wires and servos pulling loose, until he'd ripped the limb free, and then he turned the blaster on the droid, blowing its head off.

Which left him holding the severed arm.

Mando activated a switch on the thing's wiring. A key extended outward, and he plugged it into the port on the door. It drew open, and he stepped out.

It was time to go hunting.

CHAPTER

22

"COME ON!" Mayfeld shouted. "Attack fleet's on their way. We gotta go!"

Through the communicator's earpiece, Zero's voice had the same calm authority as always. "You have ten minutes remaining."

Mayfeld and the others were running down the corridor toward the exit point when the power shut off and the doors started slamming down around them. It was as if the entire prison ship had decided to seal them inside. Had the air vents started shutting down, too? Mayfeld felt a sudden flutter of claustrophobia, like a rubber glove squeezing his lungs, making it difficult to breathe.

I'm not getting trapped here, he thought. *I'll die first.*

He thought about the Mandalorian. Maybe they shouldn't have double-crossed him.

Too late now, he thought, and turned the corner.

Dead end.

Inside the command center, Mando continued to activate the ship's remote systems, shutting the doors and closing off hallways. On the video monitors, he could see Mayfeld and the others, their faces bathed in the red glow of the transport's backup power supply. Divided from each other, lost in the maze of corridors, they were starting to panic.

He closed another door.

Cut off from Xi'an and Burg, Mayfeld found himself alone with the male Twi'lek, Qin. Alarms were blaring, no doubt announcing the impending arrival of the New Republic fleet. They were running out of time.

The prisoner grinned at Mayfeld. "You got a name?"

"Mayfeld."

"Well, Mr. Mayfeld," Qin said. "You're gonna get me off this ship."

"What about your sister?" Mayfeld asked.

Qin's grin widened. "What about her?"

As the Twi'lek turned and started walking away, Mayfeld shook his head. "Nice family," he muttered.

Inside the command center, the Mandalorian bent down to retrieve the blinking tracker device that the corrections officer had activated. It occurred to Mando that if he waited, at least one of his targets would come to him.

It was Burg who burst into the command center first.

The Devaronian stood there, looking around at the consoles of blinking lights and monitor screens. He'd been ready for a fight, but the area appeared abandoned.

Then he heard the sound above.

From his hiding place overhead, Mando fired his cable down and yanked Burg off his feet, only to have the ceiling collapse under the Devaronian's weight, causing Mando to fall on top of him. Furious, Burg snarled and swung his fist at him. He was impossibly strong, and there was no way the bounty hunter could hold his own against him in a physical fight. Mando allowed himself to be picked up and hurled backward as Burg growled at him from the open doorway, preparing to finish the job.

The Mandalorian slammed the hatch down on him with a resolute clang. A moment passed, and Burg shoved the door upward, rising to his feet with a sneer of victory.

Mando hit the second button, and the side doors slammed together.

This time, Burg didn't get up.

"Man-do," Xi'an trilled, her voice taunting. "Where are you?"

Mando stepped into view. The Twi'lek female, leering with delight and displaying sharp canines, responded at once and began flinging knives at him. He ducked, moving fast, dodging the blades, and coming up underneath her. After all that time, his speed was a surprise to her.

Mando gripped her around the waist. His own dagger was in his hand, underneath her throat. Xi'an's eyes flicked to him, and she went very still.

"Go ahead," she said. "What are you waiting for?"

Mayfeld stood motionless in the darkness. He knew the Mandalorian was out there somewhere, stalking him, coming closer. Mayfeld sensed his approach, and as the light flickered overhead, he felt his nerves start to give way to panic. Sweat broke across his upper lip, and he could feel his heart pounding. His mind flashed to what he'd said earlier, taunting the Mandalorian about being paranoid.

Who was being paranoid now?

He's nearby, Mayfeld thought. *I can smell him. He's somewhere very close.* His firing arm whirled senselessly, sightless in the shadows.

The next thing he felt was a gloved hand gripping him hard.

He didn't have time to scream.

Mando found Qin on the ladder leading up to the *Razor Crest.* When the prisoner saw Mando's shadow on the wall, he stopped trying to escape and looked over his shoulder at the bounty hunter. His voice sounded resigned. "You killed the others."

"They got what they deserved," Mando said.

With a snarl, the male Twi'lek whipped around, weapon in hand. But the bounty hunter was waiting for him with a blaster already pointed at his chest.

"You kill me," Qin said, "you don't get your money." He grinned, teeth gleaming savagely. "Whatever Ran promised, I'll make sure you get it, and more." The prisoner took a step toward the Mandalorian, then another, advancing slowly, arms at his sides. "Come on, Mando. Be reasonable." He tossed his own blaster aside and held out his wrists, chuckling. "You were hired to do a job, right? Isn't that your code? Aren't you a man of honor?"

Mando didn't answer.

On board the *Razor Crest*, the Child had been enjoying his game of hide-and-seek with the droid named Zero. At least, it had *seemed* like a game at the time. But then the droid had found him, and the Child perceived that the game had turned serious. The droid had a rifle in its hands, and the rifle looked dangerous. Perhaps it wasn't just a funny game after all.

Zero pointed the blaster at the Child, and the Child raised his hand, closing his eyes. As he concentrated, his long ears drawing flat with the intensity of his focus, there was a burst of violent energy from behind the droid. A sudden explosion of sparks burst from its chest plate as it crumpled over.

The Mandalorian stood there, blaster in hand.

The Child cooed and smiled at him.

"Where are the others?" Ranzar Malk asked.

Back at the Roost, Ran had been waiting to meet the *Razor Crest* as it docked and sent down its ramp, allowing Qin to step off and meet him. As Ran greeted the prisoner with a hug, the Mandalorian looked down at the bearded man.

"No questions asked," Mando said. "That's the policy, right?"

"Yeah," Ran said. "That is the policy."

"I did the job."

"Yeah, you did." Ran tossed him a bag of credits. "Don't spend it all in one place."

"Just like the good old days," Mando said.

"Just like the good old days."

The Mandalorian walked back up the gangway and hit the switch to close the hatch. A moment later, the *Crest's* landing gear lifted from the pad as the ship began to move upward and out of the port.

Watching the ship go, Ran raised one hand, smiling and waving. He waited until the *Crest* began to move out. Then his smile disappeared. He leaned down and activated a communications line. His voice was cold, dismissive.

"Kill him."

He could hear Qin chuckling as the docking doors alongside them opened, the lift rising to bring the gunship into view. It would make quick work of the *Razor Crest*, Ran knew. Nobody would ever hear from the Mandalorian again. His good old days—*all* his days—would soon be over.

Beeping made him look over to see Qin holding a blinking device in his hand. Apparently the Mandalorian had tucked it into the Twi'lek prisoner's pocket before he'd brought him back.

"What's this?" the Twi'lek asked, holding it up.

Ran stared at the tracker in shock, realizing what it meant. Through the open hatch, he could already see the three ships from the New Republic racing toward them. They appeared to be approaching the space station at a very aggressive rate of speed.

"Are those X-wings?" Qin asked. He sounded confused.

Ran didn't have a chance to answer before the ships opened fire.

CHAPTER

"MY FRIEND." Greef Karga's image flickered to life on the ship's holoprojector. "If you are receiving this transmission, that means you are alive." The Guild agent gazed out at him, hands on hips. "You might be surprised to hear this, but I am alive, too. I guess we can call it even."

The Mandalorian watched the image carefully, listening to every word.

"A lot has happened since we last saw each other," Karga continued. "The man who hired you is still here, and his ranks of ex-Imperial guards have grown. They rule over my city, which has impeded the livelihood of the Guild. We consider him an enemy, but we cannot get close enough to take him out." Karga crossed his arms, getting right to the point. "If you would consider one last commission, I will very much make it worth your while. You have been successful so far against their hunters, but they will not stop until they have their prize. So here is my proposition. Return to Nevarro, and bring the Child as bait. I will arrange an exchange and loyal Guild members as protection. Once we get near the Client, you kill him, and we both get what we want. If you succeed, you keep the Child, and I will have your name cleared with the Guild, for a man of honor should not be forced to live in exile." Karga paused, allowing the terms to resonate in Mando's mind. "I await your arrival with optimism."

Mando switched off the transmission and turned around to look at the Child. He was fast asleep in his pram, snoring softly.

The Mandalorian turned to the navicomputer and plotted a course for Sorgan.

Fighting always made Cara Dune feel better about her life choices. Winning bets while doing it was just an added bonus.

In the time since Mando's departure, she'd been restless and bored, looking for ways to make money, preferably while blowing off steam. In the common house where bone broth was the local specialty, attached by an energy tether to a male Zabrak fighter, she'd found a way to let out her aggressions—and win a few bets.

If she survived long enough.

Wham! The Zabrak slammed her in the face, sending her backward against the bar. All around her, the crowd cheered. Stumbling, Cara shook it off and charged him, hammering him hard in the jaw and following up with a roundhouse kick to his stomach. That made him angry, and sloppy, which was precisely her goal.

"Come on!" the Zabrak snarled, grabbing the tether in both hands and pulling her across the floor toward him. Cara allowed herself to be dragged closer, letting him tire himself out with the effort. At the last second, she ducked as his fist whistled over her head, and while he was still off balance, she came back hard with a rib-cracking side punch that doubled him over.

Say hello to the floor for me, she thought.

The Zabrak grunted, sucking wind. Swinging on top of him, she grabbed the tether and wrapped it around his neck, yanking it tight until he finally deactivated his end, thudding to the floor.

The crowd applauded, roaring their approval. Panting, Cara raised her hands in victory and pointed at the ones who had bet against her. "Pay up, mudscuffers!" she cried out, and gathered the credits from their hands. "Come on, that's mine. Thank you. . . ."

As the crowd parted, she saw the Mandalorian making his way toward her.

"Looking for some work?" he asked.

Later, sitting at a table together, he outlined the operation for her, as Greef Karga had explained it to him. "They're providing the plan and firepower. I'm the trap."

Cara's eyes moved to the small, long-eared creature who was following their discussion with avid interest. "With the kid?"

"That's why I'm coming to you."

"I don't know. I've been advised to lay low." She glanced at him dubiously. "If anybody identifies me, I'll rot in a cell for the rest of my life."

"I thought you were a veteran."

"I've been a lot of things since," Cara said, thinking of the various jobs she'd done, and the hard feelings she'd left behind. "If I so much as book passage on a ship registered to the New Republic—"

"I *have* a ship," Mando told her. "I can bring you there and back with a handsome reward. You can live free of worry."

"I'm already free of worry," she said, "and I'm not in the mood to play soldier anymore." She raised her eyebrows for emphasis. "Especially fighting some local warlord."

"He's not a local warlord," Mando said. "He's Imperial."

Cara paused at that, reconsidered, and raised her cup. "I'm in."

Cara traveled light, and it didn't take long for her to pack up. Within the hour, they were aboard the *Razor Crest*, heading into space. The Mandalorian set the system for autopilot, and they went down to the ship's hold. Cara studied the onboard arsenal of blasters and explosives, deciding what weapons suited her best. They all looked good, but the thermal detonator held a particular allure. Cara weighed it in her hand.

"Whoa!" she shouted as the ship veered abruptly to the side and started to shake. Mando grabbed the wall for support and made his way up into the cockpit, where alarms were blaring and pulsing from the display. A moment later, he saw why.

The Child was sitting at the helm, where he'd taken hold of the throttle and was babbling happily, trying to steer the ship. Lunging forward, the bounty hunter managed to lift him away from the throttle and pass him back to Cara before taking over the controls. He stabilized the vessel and switched off the alarms.

Cara let out a breath. "We need someone to watch that thing."

"Yeah," Mando said.

"You got anyone you can trust?"

The Mandalorian thought he knew just the one.

Kuiil was harnessing his blurrg when he saw the familiar shape of the *Razor Crest* descending in front of his homestead. When the hatch opened, he greeted the new arrivals and led them inside. The Mandalorian was there with the Child, and another one, a fighter from the look of her.

The Ugnaught studied the Child. "It hasn't grown much," he said, and glanced at Cara. "What about this one? Does she have a name?"

"This is Cara," Mando said. "She was a shock trooper."

"You were a Dropper," Kuiil observed.

She nodded. "Did you serve?"

"On the other side, I'm afraid." Kuiil lowered himself into his seat. "But I'm proud to say that I paid out my clan's debt, and now I serve no one but myself."

The door behind him opened, and a droid stepped into the room. IG-11 was so tall that it had to bend down to clear the hatchway, but the tea tray in its hands remained perfectly level.

Seeing the bounty droid, Mando sprang to his feet, blaster in hand, and Cara joined him. IG-11 remained unperturbed.

"Would anyone care for some tea?"

"Please," the Ugnaught said, "lower your blasters. He will not harm you."

The Mandalorian kept his weapon trained carefully on the bounty droid's head. "That thing is programmed to kill the baby."

Kuiil shook his head. "Not anymore."

As Mando and Cara listened, the Ugnaught relayed the story of how he'd found the droid in the wake of the battle, devoid of all life. He had gathered the IG and loaded it onto the back of his blurrg, taking it to his workshop to assess the damage. It was extensive. Little had remained of its neural harness, and reconstruction was difficult. Once the mechanical repairs were finished, Kuiil had spent days teaching the droid everything from scratch—how to stand, how to walk, simple tasks like how to pick up a box or pour out water. It had required patience and repetition.

"I spent day after day reinforcing its development with patience and affirmation," Kuiil said as the droid poured tea for the guests. "It developed a personality as its experiences grew."

Mando was unconvinced. "Is it still a hunter?"

"No," the Ugnaught said, "but it will protect."

IG-11 raised its arm, extending a cup. "Tea?"

The Mandalorian looked at it and sighed.

Later that night, while Kuiil was feeding the blurrgs, Mando spoke to him about why he'd really come back to Arvala-7: to hire him as a protector for the Child.

"I cannot accept your offer," the Ugnaught said. "But IG-11 will serve your needs. I can reprogram him to watch over the Child."

"No," Mando said firmly. "I don't want that droid anywhere near him."

The Ugnaught blinked at him. "They are not good or bad," he said. "They are neutral reflections of those who imprint them." He straightened up and regarded the Mandalorian. "Do you trust me?"

"From what I can tell, yes."

"Then you will trust my work," Kuiil said, as if the matter was settled. "I will go with you, and IG-11 will join me. We do it not for payment, but to protect the Child from Imperial slavery." He gazed up at the Mandalorian and spoke from his heart: "None will be free until the old ways are gone forever."

There seemed nothing more to say, so Mando simply agreed. "Okay."

"The blurrgs will join me, as well."

"The blurrgs?"

"I have spoken," said Kuiil, and walked away.

The blurrgs fit nicely in the *Razor Crest*'s cargo hold, and the Ugnaught rode next to them, apparently content with their company. Once they were underway, Cara approached the Mandalorian. He was at a table near the cargo hold with the Child. She dropped a handful of credits in front of him, sat down, and extended her hand.

He looked at the credits, then up at her. "You sure you want to do this?"

Cara grinned. "You scared?"

He planted his elbow, clasped her hand, and a moment later they were both straining to push the other's arm over. Cara knew they would be pretty evenly matched, but as she pushed harder, she felt Mando starting to weaken.

"I got you, Mando."

He was grunting. "Care to double the bet?"

Cara pushed harder, her smile tightening across her face. Now she knew she was going to win, and when she did, she was never going to let him hear the end of it, especially—

Suddenly her thoughts broke off. An invisible hand seemed to be tightening around her neck, choking her. She sat bolt upright, clutching at her throat. With her vision already starting to darken around the edges, she caught a glimpse of the Child with his eyes closed, hand outstretched in her direction.

"No!" Mando shouted, and she saw him reach over and grab the Child "Stop! We're friends! Cara is my friend!"

The choking ended, and she felt herself being released. With a gasp, she sat forward and pointed at the Child. "That is *not* okay!"

The Mandalorian lowered the Child into his crib.

"Interesting," Kuiil said.

"*Interesting?*" Cara gaped at him. "That thing almost killed me!"

Mando regarded the Ugnaught. Kuiil was watching the

Child, processing what he'd just witnessed. "What you told me about the mudhorn now makes more sense," he told Mando finally.

"I could use your skills," the bounty hunter told him. "Could you modify the Child's crib with some cushions so that he sleeps better?"

"I will fabricate a better one," Kuiil said, and set to work.

Cara rubbed her throat where she'd felt the invisible hand gripping her airway. From then on, she'd be more careful around the little one.

CHAPTER

24

LANDING ON THE LAVA fields of Nevarro, they found Greef Karga waiting for them, along with a trio of local bounty hunters—a human, a Nikto, and a Trandoshan. Kuiil unloaded the blurrgs, leading them down the *Crest's* ramp, and Mando and Cara joined him to mount up and ride over to Karga.

Karga and his hunters stood their ground, watching as Mando and the others approached. "Sorry for the remote rendezvous, Mando," the Guild agent said. "But things have gotten complicated since you were last here." He spread his arms. "Now, where is the little one?"

Mando clicked a button on his wrist gauntlet, and the silver pram floated forward, opening to reveal the Child's face. At the sight of him, Karga blinked in surprise.

"So," he said, "this little bogwing is what all the fuss was about." Reaching down, he lifted the Child up. "What a precious little creature. I can see why you didn't want to harm a hair on its wrinkled little head." Replacing the Child, he looked back at Mando. "I'm glad this matter will be put to rest, once and for all. Shall we go?"

The sun dropped fast on Nevarro. They traveled for a while on foot across the lava fields, none of them speaking much, and then set up camp at the riverbank, with the intention of making their way into town at first light.

That night, as they were gathered around the campfire, Kuiil fed scraps of meat to the Child, who devoured it hungrily, smacking his lips.

"I guess the little bugger's a carnivore," Karga marveled. "Never seen anything like it." He leaned in closer. "They were ready to pay a king's ransom for that thing."

"Let's go over the plan again," the Mandalorian said.

Karga sketched out the steps. It wasn't complicated. They were going together to the public house with the Child as bait. They would join the Client at the table, where Mando would kill him. Any complications involving his accompanying team of stormtroopers—four at the most, Karga promised—would be handled by his own hunters and Cara Dune. It all sounded very straightforward.

"Trust me," Karga said, "nothing could go wrong."

The words were still on his lips when a winged creature came plunging down out of the darkness with a deafening screech. Karga cried out in shock and pain, jerking his arm away, and lurched backward as chaos overtook the camp. The bounty hunters pulled their blasters and started shooting.

"Get down!" The Mandalorian jumped up and closed the Child's pram, sealing it tight. Raising his rifle, he opened fire along with the bounty hunters and Cara Dune. It didn't seem to matter. The night erupted with screeching and the leathery rustle of wings as the reptavians, three or four of them at least, swooped down on them, greedy for the kill. One whooshed close, sinking its talons into a blurrg, which shrieked in panic.

"Drop her!" Kuiil shouted, but the thing was already pumping its wings and flying off with the blurrg.

The Mandalorian stared into the blackness, listening. Then another of the creatures dove close and seized the Trandoshan bounty hunter in its claws, ripping him from the ground. Another reptavian went after a second blurrg, and they opened fire on the thing, blasting it as it screeched and jerked at the blurrg's tough hide. Blaster fire hit the blurrg, tearing it down, and the creature collapsed as two more reptavians swung down with their talons extended. Mando raised his arm and released a jet of flame, torching the flying creatures until they gave up and flew into the night like a pair of blazing kites.

Just like that, it was over. There was no sound but the frightened whimpers of the Child as the pram opened and Greef Karga's groans of pain. The wound on his arm was deep, and the reptavian venom was notoriously fast-acting. Once it hit the bloodstream, death could come in a matter of minutes.

"Hold still." Cara sat down next to him and broke open a medpac, examining the wound. "They got you good."

"How bad?" Mando asked.

"Bad," she said. "The poison's spreading fast. This isn't working!" She glanced over at the Child, who had crawled out of his hover pram and approached her and Karga from behind. "Get this thing outta here."

"Wait," Kuiil said quietly.

Karga's eyes rolled over to the Child, who was gazing at him raptly. "He's trying to eat me!" the Guild agent said. But Karga didn't move away, and they all stood watching as the Child pressed one tiny hand directly on Karga's wound, closing his eyes and holding it there.

Gradually, Karga's groans trailed off, and he looked up in disbelief.

The wound was healing, and then—

The wound was gone.

Karga stared at the Child in utter disbelief. The only sound was the crackle of the fire as he and the others eyed each other, with no idea what they'd just seen.

As dawn broke, they traveled down out of the lava fields on the outskirts of town, a ragged party already on the verge of exhaustion from the previous night's attack. Karga and the remaining two bounty hunters he'd brought with him walked ahead while Mando and Cara followed on foot, with Kuiil astride the one blurrg that had managed to survive the night.

Cara watched as Karga conferred in murmurs with his fellow hunters in front of them. "You think they're having second thoughts?" she asked.

"Could be," the Mandalorian said. "I need your eyes."

"I'm watching."

They stopped on a bluff overlooking the town below, Karga gazing down at the city. "I guess this is it," he said without turning around. Mando and Cara paused, tensing to see what was going to happen. Mando could hear the other two bounty hunters coming up behind them, their footsteps halting, then the creak of holster leather.

All at once, Karga spun around, blasters in both hands, and fired.

He hit the two hunters—the human and the Nikto— in the chest, dropping each with a single shot. As their bodies hit the ground, he raised both guns in the air. Mando and Cara approached him from either side with their own weapons drawn and pointed at him.

"There's something you should know," Karga said grimly. "The plan was to kill you and take the kid." He looked back at them and shook his head. "But after what happened last night . . . I couldn't go through with it." He furrowed his brow. "Go on, you can gun me down here and now, and it wouldn't violate the Code. But if you do, this Child will never be safe."

Mando and Cara kept their blasters pointed at him. "We'll take our chances," Cara said.

"Perhaps you should let him speak," said Kuiil.

"We both need the Client eliminated," Karga told them. "Let me take the Child to him, and then you two . . ."

"No," Mando said, and lowered his blaster.

Cara frowned at him. "What are you doing?"

"As long as the Imp lives, he'll send hunters after the Child." He turned to Karga. "Bring me. Tell him you captured me. Get me close to him, and I'll kill him."

"That's a good idea." The Guild agent nodded. "Give me your blaster."

"This is insane!" Cara said as Mando handed his sidearm over to Karga.

"It's the only way."

"Well, I'm coming with you," she said. "I'll tell them I caught you."

"Then she can bring the Child," Karga said.

"No." Mando's voice was firm. "The kid goes back on the ship."

"But without the Child, none of this works!"

"I have a plan," the Mandalorian said, and turned to the Ugnaught. "Kuiil, ride back to the *Razor Crest* with the Child and seal yourself in. Engage ground security protocols. Nothing on this planet will breach those doors."

Kuiil nodded. "I will keep the Child safe."

Mando held out his hands so Karga could put the binders on him. "Let's go."

CHAPTER

25

THE CITY HAD CHANGED.

There seemed to be fewer people outside conducting business, and the streets felt strangely empty. Instead, stormtroopers and scout troopers on 74-Z speeder bikes lounged openly with their weapons, observing as Karga and Cara Dune approached with Mando, his hands in the binders. The hover pram levitated along between them, its lid closed tight.

"Chain code?" a scout trooper demanded.

"I have a gift for the boss," Karga said, and handed it over.

The scout trooper scanned it. "I'll give you twenty credits for the helmet."

"Not a chance," Karga said, chuckling. "That's going on *my* wall."

"On your *wall*?" the Mandalorian murmured under his breath.

"Go with it," Karga whispered back.

The scout gestured them forward. "Go ahead."

Karga nudged the bounty hunter forward, and they kept walking. More stormtroopers watched them from either side of the street as they continued toward the public house.

It wouldn't be long.

The Client rose to his feet when he saw them come in, his eyes gleaming with interest.

"Look what I brought you," Karga said. "As promised."

The old man gazed at the Mandalorian's armor, as if admiring a piece of sculpture that had been wheeled into the room for his appraisal. "What exquisite craftsmanship." He ran one hand over the helmet's visor. "It is amazing how beautiful beskar can be when forged by its ancestral artisans." After signaling the RA-7 protocol droid behind the bar, who began to make them drinks, the old man gestured at the table. "Please sit."

Karga shoved Mando roughly behind the table, and the Client settled in across from him. "It is a shame that your people suffered so," he said, "when it was all avoidable. Why did Mandalore resist our expansion?"

Mando said nothing.

"The Empire improves every system it touches," the old man continued. "Judge by any metric. Safety, prosperity, trade, opportunity, peace . . ." His expression darkened, becoming grave. "Compare Imperial rule to what is happening now. Is the world more peaceful since the revolution?"

Staring at the Mandalorian, he didn't bother waiting for a response. "I see nothing but death and chaos." His eyes drifted over to the pram that was hovering next to the table. "I would like to see the baby."

"Uh . . ." Karga held up his hand. "It is asleep."

"We all will be quiet," the Client said.

Before Karga could reply, a nearby stormtrooper walked over and whispered something into the old man's ear.

"Don't think me to be rude," he said, standing up. "I must take this call."

As he left the table, the Mandalorian detached the binders from his wrists, freeing his hands. "Give me the blaster," he whispered.

Karga slipped it to him. "You get one shot."

Over at the bar, the Client leaned forward toward the holoprojector, where the image had appeared in front of him, a lean-faced figure studying him with cold, estimating eyes.

"Yes, Moff Gideon?"

"Have they brought the Child?" Gideon asked. His voice sounded deceptively casual, almost conversational.

"Yes, they have," the old man said. "Currently, it is sleeping."

"You may want to check again."

The old man's eyes narrowed and flicked to the right, suspicion sweeping over his face.

A shot burst through the window behind the bar.

The old man went sprawling and collapsed to the floor.

The stormtroopers spun around, already firing their blasters, as chaos erupted. Across the room, Karga flipped over the table, and he and the others scrambled for cover. From the shattered window, a shaft of daylight streamed through the smoky air. The protocol droid behind the bar raised its hands and ducked for cover.

Moff Gideon's hologram observed all of this for a moment, then leaned down to deactivate his transmitter and disappeared.

After the shooting stopped, Cara got up to check the room and make sure the troopers were down. Karga and Mando joined her. Cara turned to look through the shattered window onto the street. When she saw what was out there, a sudden wave of dread flooded through her.

A row of black-armored death troopers stood in front of the public house. They were the Empire's elite forces, designed for stealth. Behind them, an Imperial troop trans-port pulled up and whooshed to a halt, its doors opening to disgorge a contingent of stormtroopers.

"This is bad," Cara said.

Mando raised the comlink to his helmet. "Kuiil, are you back to the ship yet?"

After a crackle of radio static, the Ugnaught's voice came through, sounding very far away. "Not yet."

"Get back to the ship and bail!" Mando said. "Get the kid out of here. We're pinned down!"

Receiving the transmission, Kuiil gripped the reins and rode harder, his blurrg galloping ahead over the lava fields toward the *Razor Crest*. It wouldn't be much farther, he knew. Soon he would get to the ship, and the Child would be safe.

But he wasn't the only one who'd been listening.

On the outskirts of town, two scout troopers who had been monitoring the conversation glanced up at each other, mounted their speeder bikes, and began to ride.

CHAPTER

THE OUTLAND TIE FIGHTER swept down out of the sky and descended over the street, its solar collectors retracting as it landed behind the rows of Imperial troops. Inside the public house, with their blasters raised, Mando, Karga, and Cara Dune stared out at the fighter, none of them speaking, although they all knew what it meant.

The hour of reckoning had come.

The TIE's hatch hissed open, and a man in a dark cloak and chest armor stepped out. He strode forward through the ranks of troopers, approaching the building. It was the Imperial officer from the holoprojector, the one who had been addressing the old man.

Moff Gideon.

He stopped in front of the open window and spoke in a calm, dispassionate voice. "You have something I want," he said. "You may think you have some idea of what you are in possession of, but you do not." He peered in at them with cold, self-confident eyes. "It means more to me than you will ever know. And in a few moments, it will be mine."

Mando raised the comlink. "Kuiil, are you back to the ship yet?" he asked. "They're onto us. Kuiil, come in!"

But there was no response.

Kuiil rode faster. There was no time to reply to the Mandalorian's message. He could see the *Razor Crest* ahead of him, the ship outlined clearly against the blue sky. It was just a matter of minutes, perhaps less. He urged the blurrg on, the beast running full tilt. He could hear the Child, wrapped in blankets in his arms, cooing softly.

Protect the Child, he thought. Right then, it was the most important task of his life.

Close enough that he could remotely activate the ship's security system, he hit a switch and the *Razor Crest*'s ramp began extending downward. He could actually see inside the ship's hold, the place where they would be safe.

The shriek of speeder bikes overtook him.

When the scouts fired, taking out the blurrg and throwing Kuiil forward to the ground, the Ugnaught saw the Child flying from his arms and knew the abrupt and horrible truth.

He had failed to protect the Child. The white helmets

and visors of the scouts loomed over him, as impersonal as death itself.

"No!" Kuiil raised one hand, making a final, desperate attempt to hold them off.

The blaster bolt hit him, and he knew only darkness.

CHAPTER

27

RIDING BACK TO THE CITY, the two scout troopers who had grabbed the Child slowed down and stopped on the outskirts to report back.

"Speeder bikes have arrived at the checkpoint with the asset," the first trooper said through his comlink. "Awaiting confirmation—" Inside his shoulder bag, the Child squealed, and the trooper swatted it. "Knock it off!"

"Uh, that's a go to proceed," the person on the other end of the comms responded, "but I advise you to double-check. The Moff just touched down and already took out a squad of local troopers."

The scout troopers exchanged glances, and the first one keyed the mic. "Roger that. Standing by."

After a moment, the second trooper glanced at him. "Did . . . he just say that Gideon killed his own men?"

The first trooper shook his head. "Who knows?" he said.

"These guys like to lay down the law when they first arrive into town. You know how it is." Inside the pouch, the Child gurgled, and the trooper slapped it again. "I said, shut up!"

The second trooper craned his neck for a better look at the bag, which was moving around. "What *is* that thing, anyway?"

"Ah, I don't know. Maybe Moff wants to eat it. I don't ask questions."

The second trooper looked at him. "Can I see it?"

The trooper with the pouch stared at him in disbelief. "Did you not just hear that Moff Gideon killed a dozen of his own troops just to make a point?"

"Okay—"

"I get that point. Do you get the point?"

"Yes, I get the point."

"Okay."

They sat back on their speeders, awaiting further instructions. Nothing happened. The sun beat down. After the excitement of chasing the Ugnaught and recovering the Child, time seemed to have slowed to a crawl. If there was one thing the Rebellion hadn't changed, it was that much of life was still waiting around to be told what to do.

After a moment, the second trooper sighed. He took out his blaster and aimed it down at a transmitter lying in the sand. He pulled the trigger. Missed. Fired again. Missed. The other trooper joined him, alternating shots, neither of them hitting anywhere close to the transmitter. Neither of them spoke. The second trooper glanced hopefully at the satchel.

"Should we offer that thing some water?"

The first trooper looked at him. "You just want to see it."

"*You* got to see it—"

"Just barely. I scooped it up and stuffed it in the sack."

"It's more than I got to see it—"

The first trooper sighed. "Fine," he said, and lifted the flap, opening the bag. "There, you happy?"

"Whoa." The second trooper stared down at the wrinkled, wide-eyed face peering up at him. "What is that thing?"

"I don't know, it's a pet or something."

"A pet?" He extended one finger to touch it, and the thing opened its mouth and bit him. He yelped and jerked his hand back, then punched it hard.

The first trooper shrugged. "Serves you right."

"Stop that," an automated voice said in front of them.

Both troopers grabbed their blasters and pointed them up at the shining metal form advancing toward them. "Identify yourself!"

"I am IG-11," the droid said. "I am this child's nurse droid and require that you remand him to me immediately."

"A *nurse* droid?" The second trooper glanced at his partner. "I thought it was a hunter. Aren't IGs usually hunters?"

"Well, evidently this one's a nurse," the first trooper said.

"I'm sorry, nurse, but you're gonna have to get out of here."

IG-11 continued to walk toward them. "Are you refusing my request?"

"No," the trooper said, aiming his blaster at the droid's head, "I'm telling you to get out of here."

Moving in a blur, the IG grabbed the trooper's gun hand and twisted. The trooper screamed as his wrist snapped, and the droid flipped him over and threw him on the ground. Spinning, the IG whipped around and slapped the second trooper's blaster aside, grabbed him around the neck, and began smashing his head repeatedly against the speeder bike. Then it walked over, picked up the child, and seated itself on the other speeder bike, activating its engine. The Child blinked and gazed up at him.

"That was unpleasant," IG-11 said. "I'm sorry you had to see that."

They took off.

Inside the public house, the standoff continued.

With her back against the wall, Cara glanced at Greef Karga. "Is there another way out?"

"No," Karga said. "That's it."

"What about the sewers?" Mando asked. "The Mandalorians have a hideout down in the sewers. If we can get down there, they can help us escape."

"Yeah," Cara said. "Sewers are good."

Mando switched on his scanner. "Checking for access points."

Cara stared out the open window. On the other side of the public house wall, the stormtroopers had unpacked a large white crate and were flipping its latches and raising the lid. The row of Imperial forces moved to either side as the troopers brought out a tripod and began assembling what she realized was a heavy repeating blaster. She felt a wave of hopelessness settle over her.

Karga's shoulders sagged. "It's over."

Through his visor scanner, Mando picked up a heat signature along the far wall. "I found the sewer vent," he said.

"Let's get out of here," Cara said. She and Mando grabbed the bench and pulled it loose to expose the access point. The grate underneath looked as if it had been cemented in place, and when they yanked on it, it wouldn't budge. Cara grabbed her blaster rifle. "Get out of the way!" She opened fire on the grate, but it held tight.

From outside, Moff Gideon's voice rang out clearly. "Your astute panic suggests that you understand the situation," he said. As always, his tone remained calm and reasonable. "I would prefer to avoid any further violence, and encourage a moment of consideration." He gestured at the heavy blaster resting on a tripod. "If you are unfamiliar with this weapon, I am sure that Republic shock trooper Carasynthia Dune of Alderaan will advise you that she has witnessed many of her ranks vaporize mid-descent facing the predecessor of this particular model." He paused, allowing them to process what he was saying. "Or perhaps the decommissioned Mandalorian hunter Din Djarin has heard the songs of the Siege of Mandalore, when gunships outfitted with similar ordnance laid waste to fields of Mandalorian recruits in the Night of a Thousand Tears."

Mando stared at him, motionless, listening.

"I advise disgraced magistrate Greef Karga to search the wisdom of his years," Gideon said, "and urge you to lay down your arms and come outside. The structure you are trapped in will be razed in short order, and your storied lives will come to an unceremonious end."

It was Karga who finally answered him, leaning forward and raising his voice to be heard through the open window. "What do you propose?" he called out.

Gideon's cold gaze continued, unblinking. "Reasonable negotiation."

"What assurance do you offer?"

"If you're asking if you can trust me," Gideon said, "you cannot." He spread his hands in the gesture of one conveying an unfortunate but inevitable truth. "Just as you betrayed our business arrangement, I would gladly break any promise and watch you die at my hand. The assurance I give is this: I will act in my own self-interest, which at this time involves your cooperation and benefit." He turned to survey the forces and weaponry around him, and beyond it all, the steadily sinking sun, and then looked back at the public house. "I will give you until nightfall. And then I will have the cannon open fire."

He turned and walked away.

"The minute we open that door, we're dead," Cara said.

"We're dead if we *don't*," said Karga. "At least out there we've got a shot."

"That's easy for you to say," Cara said. "I'm a rebel shock trooper. They'll upload me to a mind flayer!"

Karga snorted. "Those aren't real. That was just wartime propaganda."

"Well," she said, brandishing her rifle, "I don't care to find out. I'm shooting my way out of here."

The Guild agent looked over at the bounty hunter. "Mando, what about you?"

"I know who he is," Mando said. "That's Moff Gideon. I haven't heard that name spoken since I was a child."

Karga glanced at him. "On Mandalore?"

"I was not born on Mandalore."

"But you're a Mandalorian." Karga frowned.

Cara shook her head. "Mandalorian isn't a race."

"It's a creed," Mando said. He was thinking again about that long-ago day with his parents, running down the street, the roar of blasters and people screaming as the gunships flew over. That was the last time he'd seen them alive. The memory continued to play out in his mind: walls exploding and buildings collapsing, spraying debris and great billows of smoke as they continued to run. Behind them, super battle droids had landed, and he could hear the blasters as they cut down bystanders. He and his parents approached the bunker, swinging open the double doors. His mother clasped his shoulders and took one final look at his face; his father pulled him close to kiss his forehead, the man's tears cutting tracks in the dirt smeared on his cheeks. They looked at him one last time.

Then they lowered him inside.

He looked up, lifting one hand toward them, their faces already blocked out by the blinding light behind them. His father closed the doors, cloaking the boy in shadow.

An instant later, the explosion hit.

It was forceful enough to shake the doors on their hinges. Silt and smoke oozed through the crack. Through the gap between the doors, he could hear the footsteps of something heavy approaching, and he knew what it was—one of the super battle droids.

The doors swung open, and there it stood, massive, merciless, towering over him and threatening certain death. The droid extended its wrist blaster and aimed it point-blank at his head.

He closed his eyes and turned away, anticipating what would come next.

WHAM!

A volley of blaster fire from above smashed into the droid, blowing holes in it and knocking it sideways with a hollow clank. When he looked up again, a new figure had appeared in the doorway.

He stared up at the Mandalorian soldier reaching down to offer a hand, beckoning him to safety.

The boy stood up to join him and felt the soldier lift him out of the shelter, then plant his feet on the ground. All around him, he could see Mandalorians in jet packs, landing with their blasters out and fighting back against the Imperials. They were blasting the assassin droids from all sides—and they were *winning*. One of them gestured at the soldier who had helped him out of the bunker, making a motion for liftoff. The Mandalorian looked at him, and the boy nodded back. Taking him in his arms, the soldier activated his jet pack and took flight.

Mando remembered what it was like looking over the soldier's shoulder, down at the place where his parents had fallen, as his rescuer took him to safety.

"I was a foundling," he said to Karga and Cara. "They raised me in the fighting corps. I was treated as one of their own. When I came of age, I was sworn to the Creed. The only

record of my family name was in the registers of Mandalore."
He looked at them, saw them listening to his story. "Moff
Gideon was an ISB officer during the Purge. That's how I
know it's him."

The others didn't speak, and Mando's thoughts returned
to the Child, out there somewhere with the Ugnaught. He
activated the comlink.

"Come in, Kuiil."

Instead of the Ugnaught's voice, the familiar sound of the
Child's giggle came through the receiver. Then they heard
another familiar voice.

"Kuiil has been terminated," IG-11 said.

Mando's voice went cold. "What did you do?"

"I am fulfilling my base function," the droid said.

"Which is?"

"To nurse and protect."

IG-11 came roaring out of the desert toward the outskirts of
the city with the Child tucked safely against its chest. Coming
closer, its photoreceptors picked up a group of scout troopers
and stormtroopers at the city gate. The droid drew its blasters
and accelerated. This might also become very unpleasant,
but it had to protect the Child.

Blasting the troopers at the gate, the IG careened past
them down the street, firing nonstop from both sides at once

and taking out troopers on either side. In front of the droid, the Child giggled happily, delighted with the speed and activity, ears blowing in the wind.

Seeing the regiment of troopers ahead, the IG whirled its torso around to protect the Child and continued firing as it approached the public house.

"Look!" Cara shouted, pointing into the street as the droid arrived.

"Cover me!" Mando said. Behind him, Cara laid down a solid line of fire while the Mandalorian charged into the open, with Greef Karga not far behind him. What he saw there was even worse than he'd expected. Death troopers and stormtroopers moved to attack them. Mando and Karga fought back, firing at the helmets, kicking and punching the ones who were too close to shoot. Through the chaos, Mando could see the IG with the Child strapped to its torso, and watched as a blaster bolt hit the droid and dropped it to its knees.

Mando looked over at the heavy blaster.

Walking over, he yanked the cannon off its tripod and turned it on the remaining stormtroopers, destroying them in a rain of orange fire. Across the street, another death trooper approached the public house and placed a detonator on the wall.

Cara was still inside when the explosion blew the wall out and threw her to the ground. She grunted, trying to crawl to shelter as blaster bolts smashed into the floor and walls around her. Death troopers, two at least, were inside with her, closing in.

She sprang to her feet, rifle in hand, and shot them both down.

Out in the street, Moff Gideon watched the battle turn. His eyes narrowed slightly with distaste. This was not the outcome he'd anticipated. He aimed his blaster at the Mandalorian's helmet and squeezed off a single shot. Mando cried out in pain and shock, and swung the partially dismantled cannon in Gideon's direction. Gideon adjusted his blaster, taking aim at the power generator next to the Mandalorian, and fired.

The generator erupted in a blinding conflagration of fire and smoke, throwing Mando sideways with its impact and dropping him motionless to the ground.

From inside the public house, Cara saw him fall. She ran out past Karga, who was still firing at the troopers. Grabbing Mando's body, she dragged him back inside, with IG-11 and Karga at her heels, then slammed the door shut behind them.

Outside, Gideon felt something tighten inside his chest. Enough was enough. His patience had come to an end.

"Burn them out," he said.

CHAPTER

28

INSIDE THE PUBLIC HOUSE, Cara
Dune dragged the Mandalorian's body toward the far wall.
The bounty hunter was dead weight, and the beskar armor
only made him heavier. "Stay with me, buddy," she said.
"We're gonna get you out of here."

If he heard her, Mando didn't answer. The explosion
outside had left him unconscious and badly injured, and his
body was limp, almost lifeless. Desperately, Cara turned to
Greef Karga, who was looking at IG-11.

"This is our only way out!" the Guild agent said. "Can you
clear it?"

"Yes, of course," the droid said. It placed the Child gently on the floor and bent down to begin removing the grate,
sparks flying from the precision cutting tool in its hand.

"Yes," Karga said under his breath. "I *love* IG units."

On the floor in front of Cara Dune, the Mandalorian

stirred. His voice was weak, filled with pain, and he was struggling to breathe. "I'm not gonna make it," he said. "Go."

"Shut up," Cara said. "You just got your bell rung. You'll be fine."

"Take this." Reaching into his armor, Mando pulled out a necklace with the image of a mythosaur skull and handed it to her. "When you meet up with my tribe, show them this. Tell them the Child was in my protection. They'll give you safe passage."

Cara took the necklace and tucked it away. She put her hand along the underside of his helmet and looked down at her fingertips. They were covered with blood. "I'm gonna need to take this thing off."

"No." He grabbed her hand. "You leave me." He was gasping for air, lungs rattling. "You make sure . . . the Child is safe. . . ."

Cara started to answer him when a huge jet of flame erupted through the public house with a roar, igniting the bar and the walls. She could already feel the heat rising around her, sucking up oxygen, as the fire grew.

"I can hold them off long enough for you to escape," Mando said. "Let me have a warrior's death."

Cara stared down at him, defiant. "I won't leave you!"

"This is the Way," the Mandalorian said.

The entire building was awash in flames that began

consuming everything around them. Cara's eyes stung with smoke, and she felt her throat beginning to tighten. When she looked over at the doorway, she saw the red-striped incinerator stormtrooper stepping inside with a flamethrower. She could remember fighting their kind in the war and was all too familiar with the terrible power of the weapon in his hands.

The trooper turned and aimed the flamethrower directly at them, preparing to unleash another blast. There was nowhere to run.

This is how it ends for us, she thought. *Fighting the war all over again, in a bar on some backwater planet—*

In the corner of her eye, Cara saw the Child standing up, lifting his hands, and closing his eyes in deep concentration. What happened next was impossible, and if she hadn't seen it with her own eyes, she never would've believed it.

The fireball swept toward them with a deafening whoosh—and then, somehow, it *stopped,* as if frozen in place, its power and ferocity held at bay by the Child's powers. Cara and Greef Karga stared at it in frank astonishment. Even the Mandalorian managed to lift his head and look, the orange reflection of flames flickering off the visor of his helmet.

With a simple gesture of his hand, the Child caused the fire to swerve around and recoil on itself, engulfing the stormtrooper in a wash of heat and blowing him out through the open doorway. Distantly, they heard him scream.

Across the room, IG-11 gave the sewer grate one final

kick, and it came loose, opening up their escape. "We have to go, now!" Karga shouted.

The Mandalorian gazed up at Cara. "Go . . ." he croaked, and fell silent.

He slumped to the floor. Cara saw the IG coming toward her, handing her the satchel with the Child inside it.

"Escape and protect this child," the droid said. "I will stay with the Mandalorian."

She stood up. "Promise me you'll bring him."

"You have my word."

Cara took hold of the Child and followed Greef Karga down into the sewers, leaving IG-11 alone with Mando. She hoped she could trust the droid.

Then again, she didn't have much of a choice.

CHAPTER

29

THE PUBLIC HOUSE had become a blazing cauldron of fire, teetering on the verge of total collapse. Flames were rising higher all around them, burning out of control. The droid knelt down in front of the bounty hunter.

"Do it," Mando said.

IG-11's red processing array blinked inquisitively. "Do what?"

"Just get it over with," Mando said. "I'd rather you kill me than some Imp."

"I told you, I am no longer a hunter. I am a nurse droid."

"IGs are all hunters."

"Not this one," the droid insisted. "I was reprogrammed. I need to remove your helmet if I am to save you." It extended one hand toward the bounty hunter's helmet, and Mando lifted his blaster and pointed it at the droid.

"Try it, and I'll kill you," he said. "It is forbidden. No

living thing has seen me without my helmet since I swore the Creed."

"I am not a living thing," IG-11 said calmly. Without waiting for permission, it began detaching the helmet. There was a soft hissing sound as the helmet unsealed and came loose, and the droid lifted it off and looked at the human beneath it.

The bounty hunter's face was bloody and stricken with pain, sweat matting the dark hair against his temples and forehead. His brown eyes looked vulnerable and exposed, the gaze of a man about to greet life's last great mystery.

"This is a bacta spray," IG-11 said, extending the medical applicator along his wounds. "It will heal you in a matter of hours. You have suffered damage to your central processing unit."

"You mean my brain?" Mando said.

"That was a joke," the droid said. "It was meant to put you at ease."

Mando chuckled weakly and groaned. Then he closed his eyes.

Down in the sewers, the Child had begun crying softly. The air was damp, and dark enough that they could hardly see more than ten meters in front of them. Cara shined her light down the long tunnel ahead and stopped walking.

"What is it?" Greef Karga asked.

She held up one hand and cocked her head to listen. Footsteps were approaching in the distance, coming up behind. She and Karga turned to see who it was.

IG-11 emerged from the shadows. Limping along beside the droid, scarcely able to stand, was the Mandalorian. A light from his helmet pierced through the gloom. He looked weak, but he was at least upright and moving.

Cara ran up to him and held him up. "I got you."

They kept walking. "Do you know which way to go?" Cara asked.

"No," Mando admitted. "I don't know these tunnels."

Karga squinted into the darkness. "If we follow the smell of sulfur, it will lead us to the lava river."

"The Imps will catch us before we make the ship," Mando said. "We need the Mandalorians to escort us to safety."

He searched for tracks. The IG's bacta infusion had begun to work, and he felt stronger, able to stand and walk on his own. Moving faster, Mando led them down another corridor and around a corner, then stopped abruptly.

A pile of Mandalorian armor and helmets lay on the floor in front of him. Mando stared down at them and dropped to one knee, lifting up a random face shield and peering at it.

"We should go," Cara said.

"You go. Leave the ship." His voice was adamant. "I can't leave it this way." He turned to Greef Karga, feeling the anger building up in him. "Did you know about this? Is this the work of your bounty hunters?"

"It was not his fault," came a female voice from behind them.

Mando stopped and looked around as the Armorer stepped out of the shadows.

"It was not his fault," she said. "We knew what could happen if we left this place. The Imperials arrived shortly thereafter." She gazed down at the pile of armor and helmets. "This is what resulted."

"Did any survive?" Mando asked.

"I hope so. Some may have escaped off-world."

He looked at her. "Come with us."

"No," she said. "I will not abandon this place until I have salvaged what remains."

Mando and the others watched as she began gathering up pieces of armor. They followed her to her forge, where she took the armor in a pair of tongs and held it over the blue jets of flame. "Show me the one whose safety deemed such destruction."

"This is the one," Mando said, showing her the Child.

"This is the one that you hunted, then saved?"

"Yes," he said, and then added, "The one that saved me, as well."

She gazed at the Child, who peered up, cooing, from under the flap of the bag. "It looks helpless," she observed.

"It is injured," Mando said, "but not helpless. Its species can move objects with its mind."

The Armorer did not seem surprised. "I know of such things. The songs of eons past tell of battles between Mandalore the Great and an order of sorcerers called Jedi that fought with such powers."

"It is an enemy?"

"No," she said. "Its kind were enemies, but this individual is not." She looked at the Child again. "It is a foundling. By Creed, it is in your care." Leaning forward, she began carefully ladling the molten beskar into its mold. "You have no choice. You must reunite it with its own kind."

"Where?"

"This, you must determine."

Mando stared at her. "You expect me to search the galaxy for the home of this creature and deliver it to a race of enemy sorcerers?"

"Until that time, or it comes of age, it is in your care. You are as its father."

"Father?"

"This is the Way." The Armorer nodded. "You have earned your signet." Walking forward, she affixed the mudhorn signet to his right pauldron. "You are a clan of two."

"Thank you," Mando said. "I will wear this with honor."

A distant explosion echoed in the outer corridor.

"A scouting party," the Armorer said. "You should go." She turned to the droid. "IG, please guard the outer hallway."

The droid turned and handed the Child to Cara, who took it awkwardly. "Hang on. I don't do the baby thing," she said, but the Child squealed happily in her arms.

The Armorer returned her attention to the Mandalorian. "I have one more gift for your journey," she said. "Have you trained in the Rising Phoenix?"

"When I was a boy," Mando said.

"Then this," she said, turning to give him the jet pack, "will make you complete."

"Thank you," he said. Outside, the explosions and blasters had grown louder and closer. Mando glanced over at Cara and Greef Karga. They had restocked their ammo, but could no longer afford to stay there. It was time to go.

When they were gone, the Armorer knelt down before her forge. She made herself very still and listened to the footsteps of stormtroopers as they approached from behind—five of them, she estimated. Even as they grew near enough to touch her, she remained absolutely motionless.

"Hey, Mando," one of them said. "Where are they?" He banged the muzzle of his blaster against her helmet. "I said, where are they?"

What happened next took less than twenty seconds. The

Armorer swung her hammer hard, smashing him in the face, then spun and drove it into the helmet of the trooper opposite her. In her other hand, the chisel flew out and crashed into the third trooper's chest while she grabbed the fourth and shoved him headfirst into the blue jets of fire. When the trooper in front of her sprang up again, firing wildly, she grabbed him and spun him around so his blaster took out the attacker behind him. Dropping him, she brought the hammer down again. This time the trooper stayed down.

The room fell silent. She looked at the bodies surrounding her and felt nothing but a small but vital sense of peace, the tiniest bit of order restored.

She approached the forge, preparing to clean off her tools and return to work.

CHAPTER

MANDO AND THE OTHERS followed the tunnel to the river, which flowed toward the lava flats. As they walked, the smell of sulfur grew steadily stronger, along with the heat. At the river's edge, bubbling lava surrounded the boat. The vessel didn't appear to have been used in a very long time and remained stubbornly attached to the shore. The ferry droid sat silent, its circuits apparently fried, while Mando and Karga struggled to push the boat free.

"You guys mind getting out of the way?" Cara asked. Shifting the Child to one arm, she raised her rifle and opened fire along the riverbank, blasting the hardened lava until the vessel broke loose, bobbing in the stream. They all climbed in.

Alerted by the disturbance, the ferry droid whirred to life, its processors blinking and brightening in recognition of its passengers. It rose up on long legs until it stood towering over them in the stern of the boat, paddle in hand, and chirped out an inquiry.

"I believe he is asking where we would like to go," IG-11 said.

"Downriver," Karga said, "to the lava flat."

The droid set to work and began to paddle. Orange liquid fire sloshed around them on either side as the boat moved slowly forward. Mando saw strange, red-eyed creatures scurrying in the darkness along the banks.

"That's it!" Karga pointed at the light up ahead. "We're free!"

Mando activated his helmet scanner. "No," he said. He looked at the outlines of at least a dozen figures clustered outside, on either side of the exit point, waiting in silence. "Stormtroopers. They're flanking the mouth of the tunnel. They must know we're coming."

"Stop the boat!" Cara said. "Droid! I said stop the boat!" She pointed her blaster at the ferry droid's processing array and pulled the trigger. The droid's head burst apart in a shower of sparks, and it fell still and stopped paddling. But it didn't matter. The boat continued to move forward in the lava flow surrounding it.

IG looked in the direction of the stormtrooper platoon. "They will not be satisfied with anything less than the Child," the droid said. "This is unacceptable. I will eliminate the enemy, and you will escape."

Mando looked at the droid. "You don't have that kind of firepower, pal. You wouldn't even get to daylight."

"That is not my objective," IG-11 said. "I still have the security protocols from my manufacturer. If my designs are compromised, I must self-destruct."

"What are you talking about?" Mando asked.

"I am not permitted to be captured. I must be destroyed." The droid faced the bounty hunter. "Sadly, there is no scenario where the Child is saved in which I survive."

"No," Mando said, "you're not going anywhere. We need you."

"Please tell me the Child will be safe in your care."

"But you'll be destroyed—"

"And you will live," the IG said, "and I will have served my purpose." It looked at the Mandalorian. "There is nothing to be sad about. I have never been alive."

"I'm not . . . sad," Mando said.

"Yes, you are. I'm a nurse droid. I've analyzed your voice." IG-11 reached down and ran its mechanized finger over the Child's face, almost tenderly.

Then it turned and stepped out of the boat, into the hissing river of molten lava.

CHAPTER

31

MANDO AND THE OTHERS stood in the boat, watching as IG-11 waded through the lava, making its way toward the exit. Outside the mouth of the tunnel, the platoon of stormtroopers moved forward, blasters pointed at the droid as it stepped into daylight.

"Manufacturer's protocol dictates that I cannot be captured," the IG said, and the detonator implanted inside its body began beeping rapidly. "I must be destroyed."

The blinking light on the detonator went solid red.

The explosion was huge.

As the boat drifted out of the tunnel, Mando looked at the bodies of stormtroopers sprawled on either side of the riverbank in the drifting smoke. The droid had done it. Giving its own life, it had saved them.

A scream came across the sky. Mando jerked his head up to see the TIE fighter roaring toward them.

"Moff Gideon!" Cara shouted, and raised her blaster. Mando and Karga joined her in shooting at the fighter as it looped overhead, the ship's cannons pouring down fire on them.

"He missed!" Karga said.

"He won't next time," said Mando, watching as the TIE banked and prepared to come around again.

"Hey," Karga said, "let's make the baby do the magic hand thing." He looked hopefully over at the Child, wiggling his fingers. "Come on, baby! Do the magic hand thing!"

The Child looked at him and waved, cooing.

Karga sighed. "I'm out of ideas."

"I'm not," Mando said. He picked up the jet pack the Armorer had given him and reached around, attaching it. They could see Moff Gideon's TIE fighter heading back toward them, cannons blazing.

Activating the jets, the Mandalorian flew straight up in the air, allowing the TIE to pass underneath him. He fired his grappling cable, affixing himself to the fighter, and felt it jerk him forward hard, swinging him across the open sky.

Mando hit the jet pack again, propelling himself forward, and landed on the fighter's cockpit dome, looking straight down at Gideon's startled face. Gideon's mouth twisted in a mixture of rage and determination. Mando pointed his blaster at the hatch and fired, but the cockpit door held.

Gideon yanked hard to the left, tilting the ship sideways

and throwing Mando off the cockpit as the fighter went spiraling. The bounty hunter grunted, sliding down to the left connector of the fighter and holding on with everything he had. He pulled a detonator from his belt and snapped it in place on the connector.

Then he let go.

Below, Cara and Greef Karga watched as the entire left side of Moff Gideon's TIE fighter exploded, sending the ship off balance and careening to the ground, where it burst into a distant cloud of smoke.

A moment later, the Mandalorian dropped down in front of them, landing in a slight crouch and then rising up with a sigh.

Karga and Cara walked toward him. "That was impressive, Mando," the Guild agent said. "Very impressive." He nodded. "It looks like your Guild rates have just gone up."

"Any more stormtroopers?" the Mandalorian asked.

"I think we cleaned up the town," Cara said. "I'm thinking of staying around just to be sure."

"You're staying here?" Mando asked.

"Well, why not?" Karga said. He gestured toward the city. "Nevarro is a very fine planet, and now that the scum and villainy have been washed away, it's very respectable again."

"As a bounty hunter hive?"

Karga gave him a sidelong look. "Some of my favorite

people are bounty hunters. And perhaps"—he reached out and put a hand on Cara's shoulder—"this specimen of soldier might consider joining our ranks. And you, my friend"—he returned his attention to Mando—"you will be welcome back into the Guild with open arms."

Mando looked down at the Child, who was staring up at him, arms spread. The bounty hunter bent down and lifted him, cradling him against his chest. "I'm afraid I have more pressing matters at hand."

Cara leaned forward and touched the Child's ear. "Take care of this little one."

"Or maybe," Karga added, "it'll take care of you."

Mando nodded, turned, and ignited the jet pack. He lifted off, feeling the Child in his arms turn his head to look back down at the receding landscape, and the two figures standing there, watching them go.

Back at the *Razor Crest*, Mando buried Kuiil and left his helmet and goggles as a monument where the Ugnaught had fallen. He carried the Child on board the ship, powered it up, and got the engines firing.

The Child sat behind him, sucking on something. Mando realized that it was the mythosaur necklace he'd given Cara before they went down into the sewers. The Child had somehow ended up with it around his neck.

Mando gently pulled the mythosaur out of the Child's

mouth. "I didn't think I'd see this again," he said, then put it back in the Child's hand. "Why don't you hang on to that?"

The Child put it back in his mouth.

The *Razor Crest* lifted up and took off.

A moment later, they were gone.

It didn't take long for the Jawas to discover the wreckage of the TIE fighter. Even with the damage, there was much to salvage, and they started prying off pieces of it, getting ready to carry them away.

A sudden crackling sound erupted from within.

The Jawas let out startled cries and scattered as the laser blade sliced through the cockpit from the inside. It carved out a vaguely rectangular piece of metal, which burst loose.

A moment later, Moff Gideon stepped out, with the Darksaber in hand.

He climbed to the top of the fighter's cockpit and stood with the saber blazing in his grasp, surveying the land around him with cold and watchful eyes.

Things have changed, he thought.

But the situation was not without possibilities.

He had much work to do.